MARTIN MALONE is a novelist and short story writer. He won the John B. Keane/*Sunday Independent* Literary Award and was nominated for the International IMPAC Dublin Literary Award. He is a columnist with the *Leinster Leader*.

The Only Glow of the Day

Also by

MARTIN MALONE

Novels

The Silence of the Glasshouse
The Broken Cedar
After Kafra
Us

Memoir

The Lebanon Diaries: An Irish Soldier's Story

Radio Plays

Rosanna Night-walker
Song of the Small Bird
The Devil's Garden

Short Stories

The Mango War & Other Stories

The Only Glow of the Day

MARTIN MALONE

NEW ISLAND

THE ONLY GLOW OF THE DAY
First published 2010
by New Island
2 Brookside
Dundrum Road
Dublin 14

www.newisland.ie

ISBN 978-1-84840-077-1

Book design by Inka Hagen
Cover design by Someday

Printed and bound in the UK by CPI Mackays, Chatham ME5 8TD

10 9 8 7 6 5 4 3 2 1

SEPTEMBER, 1863

DUBLIN

HER EYES rested on the oblong patch of pale gold on the maple floor, cast there by the yellow robe of St Peter in the stained-glass window. According to the shift of light drawn so by the clouds, the refraction came and went, the colour reminding her of honeysuckle in the garden of a home where she used to live with her parents and little sister. She smelled the misty morning scent of the flowers – then this hold of the past was gone, snatched at by the present: the swing open and close of a heavy door, the sturdy and tinny noise of hobnails on the wooden floor. Another of God's wandering souls in from the searching cold and showery weather to garner heat from candle flame, if not solace.

She lifted her head and looked at heaven's letters shimmering on the tiered stand. The teardrop-sized flame of the candle she had lit was a strong and vibrant plea to the heavens: for help, for guidance, for comfort, for the journey. Blessings. I'm a true believer in times of want, she thought. At first she had prayed for nature to be kind to her and start the flow: nine weeks of saying prayers and no reply. At least not the one she'd wanted.

There was no doubt in her mind. Not now. How could there be? How long was she going to hope and pray that she was not with child? Till the baby arrived and was suckling at her breast? She smiled at the very notion – slowly shaking her head in self-chiding. What have I to worry about? she thought.

Hadn't Johnny made her promise not to be turning her head with worry? She missed him but she didn't want to begin her life with him like this: no time to themselves. Yet the child would be a sign to the world of their love for each other. So that couldn't be a bad thing. Could it?

She was to make sure and come down, he had said. No idle talk, he said earnestly, finger-wagging; I mean what I say, Rosanna, follow me down. I'll be waiting for you. He had under his arm his fur hat that the soldiers called a Busby and it had a side plume of trimmed feather, dyed blue above and green below. He had been stationed in the Royal barracks, not far from the train station. She thought it a great pity that they hadn't left him there. It was handy: it had been lovely knowing that he was not so far away. Although fearful at her plight she was also a little excited at the prospects. She'd always wanted to have children and had enjoyed nursing her mistress Flo's latest, so much so that it put her head in a dream world where deep down she knew she would never visit this side of life. Still, it was nice to dream. It would also be pleasant, given the right circumstances, to be with child. A boy, she hoped. And the right circumstances – well, she had only to announce her condition to Johnny for it to be so.

Thank God he isn't just a mouthpiece, Rosanna thought, as she genuflected before turning her back to the altar. In the vestibule she dipped her fingers in the stoup and crossed herself. Kiss of Christ cold on her forehead. Through the open doors she saw a pair of gannets flying above the river parapets. The stink of the Liffey at low tide breezed to her nostrils; another thing to be well shot of.

He'd said she was to write and let him know the time and date of her arrival and that was done a fortnight. No word back but that says nothing definite about anything. If the blood had come she would have stayed with Flo and saved a bit of money before travelling. But there'd been an act of providence: yesterday morning at first light she'd gotten up for work and while walking the carpeted hallway to the pantry saw a spill of coins at her feet. Her breath froze. Eleven shillings and four pence. She hurried the money into her apron pocket and said nothing about her discovery though she was of a strong mind to and had twice come close to telling her mistress. She held back, for she no longer saw Flo in the same light. If Flo found out she was pregnant, she'd be out the door, that's for bleddy sure.

Look at poor, poor Martha. Pegged out the door by Flo's husband after the mistress had a word in his ear about Martha's swell. Deaf ear turned to poor Martha's cries; her clothes and money owed to her thrown her way on the cobbled street, coins landing in fresh horse dung and others dancing on the worn cobbles before collapsing, her fingers picking among the horseflies to pinch her miserly earnings, hurrying then to light on the dancing coins before others seized the opportunity. She knew what happened when you let something valuable go beyond your reach. Next she gathered her garments dressing the flagstones, jamming them into a large cotton bag that had thick wooden handles. Rosanna had been drawn to the bedroom window by the commotion and watched the incident in near shock. Her heart reached out to Martha. By the time she'd descended the flights of stairs and run out the door, her friend was gone out of sight. In the hallway Flo had said, 'This is a good house, Rosanna; you'd do well to remember that.'

What Rosanna remembered most was how well Flo and Martha had gotten along, always sharing jokes and secrets – how could she possibly turn like that? Father was right, she supposed; there are two sides to every face.

She knew little of the Curragh, only what she had overheard spoken by those gentlemen who came into the city from there on business and spent the night in the guesthouse. Johnny wasn't wise to it either but what he'd heard from other soldiers who had been stationed on the camp didn't charm him to the prospects of engaging with his new posting. She'd heard it said that all sorts of winds met on the plains: cold, bitter, hard, mild, sour and kind, strong and weak. It seemed to her that it was a stretch of landscape that never knew rest. But sure, it couldn't be much worse a spot than this place, she said to herself, hastening to the train station before the next shower came pelting.

Chapter 2

HE WALKED along the wet deck of the *Mary-Louise,* a boiled sweet in his mouth, sucked slowly to smallness in accordance with the instructions written on the side of the tin. He broke it down into tiny shards and swallowed these: a mint to freshen his breath and perhaps settle his stomach, as the vendor had extolled, though Richard Tone very much doubted the man's veracity regarding his product. Still, it does one good, he thought, to every now and then express a hope in something that is apparently hopeless.

He didn't like anyone to make eating noises or pick at their nose or teeth while in his company as these habits grated on his nerves. Polite and restrained by nature, he said nothing to the offender, for even the mildest reproach would cause umbrage and create a void between him and those who, but for their displays of vulgarity, were really decent beings. Also, he could spend his life addressing those who had strummed his nerves. In such a circumstance he moved away and if this was not possible, he walked his mind to a different place by furling and unfurling his fingers in a form of self-hypnosis (this clenching he was not aware of till it was pointed out to him last May by his cousin Josie).

Although these habits jarred his nerves and made him impatient and irritable, he was also thus lately because of a nagging pain in his lower abdomen, a fretfulness that was unusual to his nature, as was the lassitude that he had tried in vain for some weeks to shake off. There was, he had come to believe, something amiss within the vault of his being. Ignoring and hoping and wishing it better had not worked, for the pain, though it often diminished, refused to be ignored and hoped and wished against. The notion had occurred to him to see Mr Dickens, his employer, and explain the situation, ascertain whether Dickens would hold an objection to him if he delayed his visit to Ireland by a week or so to enable a physician take stock of his ailments and diagnose a remedy. He had lost weight and become delicate in himself. His blue eyes in the mirror seemed to cry out to him. But his employer smothered the very idea before he had time to bring it to the surface. Charles said he was looking forward to reading his despatches and Richard nodded tamely. He supposed that the plight of the women could not afford a delay, and apart from this aspect there existed the danger that another newspaper might get in first to publish the story.

He watched the evening changes in the skies. The touch of blood orange on wooded hills sinking from view; the noise of scavenging gulls; the creaking and groaning sway of the vessel, like riding the sea was a torture for its timbers. He watched the first stars showing and also a slip of new moon, blemished occasionally by black smoky clouds at quick flight.

Facing into the wind, he allowed it to wash over his face, the salt air stinging a spot where the razor had cut that morning – a small mole above his lip which he had always been careful to avoid while shaving; it had taken an inordinate spell for the bleeding to stop and for a longer while still he mused over his unusual lapse into carelessness. Perhaps he ought to grow a moustache again. It made him older than his years according to his women friends, the dearest of them.

The air turned cold. Sharp. Listening to the push of wind into the belly of canvas sails, the passing chatter of other passengers, the sight of a small boy sporting gobbets of phlegm over the rail into the sea, he decided to go below deck and enjoy a brandy in his cabin. He hoped he would not meet with that insufferable cavalry officer or the pompous tea merchant or the vendor of potions and lotions whom he'd encountered earlier over light refreshments in the captain's dining room. A trio ripe with boasts, full of their own importance.

Later, if not too set against the notion, he would dip his quill in ink and perhaps write a few sentences on the stories that had emanated from Ireland about the women who lived in furze bushes and serviced the sexual avarices of soldiers from the nearby military camp, compose a questionnaire so as to not come away and later discover he had forgotten to ask this and that of them. He never forgot to ask his subject matter the most pertinent of questions but of late he was less than sure of himself. He felt too brittle within his soul to be confident about much.

Wren women, they were called.

He stifled a yawn; he felt as tired as the fabric in the age old Persian rug draped on a wall above the stairwell of his London apartment. A cultural aspect of another civilization. It was not lost on him that he was sailing a short distance to a different culture. Though long part of the empire and his kingdom's nearest neighbour, the differences between each were a far wider breach than many imagined to be the case.

Taking to the wooden steps that led to the lower decks, a solder's hefty shoulder collided with his elbow as they passed, knocking him off one foot and causing him to find balance. No apology from the ruffian, not even a backward glance to see if he had harmed another. He probably scarcely noticed the collision.

It is how some of us are, he thought sourly; we do likewise to our colonies and then wonder why is it they rebel.

As he steadied himself on the wet floorboards a bite came suddenly to the wind, bringing several sideward lurches that were quite violent but not the worst he had experienced. Other voyages had left him badly shaken and as green-faced as swamp waters.

Heavy squalls and the pitch of the vessel worked to empty the contents of stomachs into fire-buckets of sand hanging from nails driven into posts on the ship's walls. A major pitch then a slight one and the vessel seemed to find a smooth road to travel in the waters. Candle flames in lanterns that had dimmed now flourished. The watch-bell sounded. All was well. The voices that had fallen silent grew strong, too. Prayers waned in intensity. And rising above the dying chant was a woman's loud cackle and the cough of a man that suggested he was going home to die.

He heard their utterances as he passed between their silhouetted ranks: ship ghosts, standing room only on board if you were not in posession of a full purse. The stench of unwashed bodies, of vomit, reached to his nostrils and he felt bile rise up his throat as he made his way to the cabin. A climb of three steps and past the sailor guarding the cabins from invasion, he turned his key in the door. A haven here: the world at his back. What had risen to his mouth he eased into a handkerchief – the taste of one's inner self – then he sipped brandy from a hip-flask to rid his mouth of the foulness.

In the frugal comfort of his own space he leaned his back against the door and closed his eyes. Felt for his pain, rubbed at the spot. Thought of his mother – how, when he was a child, she would nurse away his ailments with kind words, the application of ointments and copious amounts of liquid: goat's milk for asthma, cough elixirs and any tonic advocated by street pedlars who swore they would have been long dead but for the contents of their bottles. His father, God be not wise to him but good, in the end forbade his mother from buying these concoctions, 'from the sewer, woman, for all we know, aye. And you pouring it into our lad.'

'Sometimes they work,' she said, 'sometimes.'

Kindly-spoken words, a father's concern, these helped with the pain: the distractions of pleasant memories a comforting anodyne.

Chapter 3

A PENNY a mile, her train fare. She walked past the first class railway compartments, glanced into one and saw a gentleman stowing his top hat in a rack. Must be great to be rich, she thought, must be. The carriages were crammed with soldiers and so the porter directed her to a goods wagon where a young lad with warts on his fingers helped her to climb aboard. He wore no shoes and the corner of his big toenail was badly infected. When she was in he jumped down and loped along the platform, hands buried in the pockets of his short trousers, giving a hobble every few strides whenever his toenail pinched.

Her eyes took moments to adjust to the semi-darkness, her nostrils quickest to familiarise with the dank smells of hay, baling twine and chicken dirt. Hens and chickens in wooden boxes secured with net wire, bales of hay bound by thick brown twine. Next to these a grey-haired man smoked a clay pipe, seemingly oblivious to the danger of spark and dry hay. Stacks of tea chests holding delft for a big house down the country. Rolls of hessian sacking atop sheets of corrugated iron and timber boarding.

A crowd of eyes and silent tongues danced on her and then they left her alone to go about what they were doing before she had arrived: talking about people, drawing comfort from a man's misfortune and a woman's worse.

The distance was short, so Johnny had said.

'Not far at all.'

It rained. And the wind would carve bone.

Leaving little to go to nothing, Flo had said to her. Oh, it wasn't for the love of me that neither she nor her husband wanted me to go; it was because they'd a skivvy less to do their washing and ironing and to cook for the farmers who arrived early mornings from Rush to sell their produce. When she'd asked Flo for her pay she had it on the tip of her mind to tell her about her find of coins but Flo's expression had turned hard and her words were bitter, 'After all I have done for you, Rosanna – now you show your lack of good breeding. You're leaving us high and dry at a busy time.'

Rosanna said, through a swell of anger, 'My pay, Miss, if you please.'

She moved her eyes to the corner of the goods wagon, to something a glimpse of sunlight had momentarily lighted upon.

A coffin.

Varnished. Full or empty? she asked herself, as a shiver touched the base of her spine. Isn't it standing upright, you fool? Empty, of course. A lone coffin. Why so? Oh, she thought, catching sight of a few more hidden from her initial sweep of eye.

She eased herself onto a tea chest. Her clothes were damp, for she had been caught in a shower on the way to the station. She left without her rags, for Johnny said he'd have a queen's apparel waiting for her in their place. She hadn't a shred of decent clothing to her name except for what she had on: a pleated black skirt, a white blouse with voluminous sleeves rolled back to form two long cuffs, a green bodice threaded with patterns of black flowers, a wine shawl and brown shoes with dodgy buckles.

The only thing of real value that she owned in the world was a gold locket and chain given to her by her father. It had belonged to her mother and was more often in the possession of a pawn shop than on her person. A small portrait of her mother inside – you and your mother, so alike, her father had said. It was something she wore around her neck and hidden behind clothing for she knew it was expensive; it had been handed down to her father from his grandfather who had fought the rebels in 1798 and took it from the neck of a croppy woman at Gibbet Rath, no doubt stolen from a Protestant homestead. It had etchings of entwined roses on its oval lid and these she often touched as one would a crucifix, almost without thought, instinctive, as a drowning man's hand might clutch at air.

A whistle sounded in long, tinny blasts. A man with a green flag slid home the carriage door. Through the thin gaps between the slats she saw him wave his flag, his cheeks sinking in as he drew once more on his whistle.

She hated its noise and yet loved what it signalled. Soon she'd be with Johnny. In hardly any time at all.

Hissing and cloud of steam, the train eased from the station in a series of jolts, slowly building speed. And then on the track, the rhythm of the train's motion lulled her into a dream world. She was vaguely aware of her clothes drying into her and it was not an altogether unpleasant sensation. She dreamed of a baby – her baby, alive inside her, part of her…

'Are you going far, Miss?' The voice strong and husky; it was the pipe-man.

She looked at him and said, 'Pardon?'

'I said, are you going far?'

'The Curragh.'

'The Curragh,' he said, drawing on the long thin shaft of his pipe and exhaling a cloud of smoke that his eyes squinted at, as though to see if anything belonging to him was being carried away.

He wiped his snub nose with the back of his hand and then looked at her without uncrossing his ankles or turning to her full on.

'What part?' he said.

She did not know for sure. 'The camp,' she said, putting certainty into her tone.

'The camp.'

He nodded, smacked his lips, and said, 'I used to soldier, Miss – that's a cold place for man, woman and beast.'

'All places are in winter,' she said.

'That neck of the woods especially.'

'I see.'

One of the women interrupted, 'Don't mind him love – it's the same as anyplace else on this earth if you're poor.'

The old man shook his head. 'The devil's breath is on that spot of land.'

'It is in its arse,' said the woman. ''Tis the acres of St Brigid and no finer woman or saint ever lived. If you don't know that then you know nothing.'

Then the woman turned her back and reimmersed herself in conversation with her friends, picking up on a morsel of news that the others thought had passed her by. A woman who missed nothing.

The old man stared at Rosanna for moments and then averted his eyes to the upright coffin. It was in neither to speak to the other again. A fit of small coughing came to her and she tried to stop it by tamping her fingers to her lips. Her eyes watered.

'I've dragged my fill for now anyhow, Miss,' said the man quietly, smothering the squat chimney of his pipe with sawdust he had pinched from the floor.

As they neared the siding after passing Newbridge station, a great excitement surged through her. She could hardly contain herself. Johnny. His smile, his easy way of talking, his gentleness, his height, his warm and strong embrace – and just wait till he hears her news. Jigs and reels, he'll do.

The train shuddered to a stop; steam hissed and belched voluminous clouds of white steam. The pipe-man slid back the door and lowered himself to the ground as the goods carriages had fallen short of the platform. He held up his hands and she allowed them to fit around her waist.

'Not a pick on you,' he said, smiling, his few teeth tobacco-stained.

'Thanks,' she said.

'Your bag, Miss,' he said, looking over her shoulder at the floor.

'Oh, I had none.'

He nodded, a frown growing on him, and climbed aboard, 'Mind yourself, Miss.'

'I will,' she said.

She pulled her thin wine shawl around her head. The wind carried the rain to her face. She felt herself getting wet through. Her shoes chafed her heels. She could almost feel the pain before it had actually begun to occur. Along the crowded platform she walked, weaving between people. She craned her neck to see where Johnny might be standing, imagining him looking at his timepiece, shaking his head, a worry line impressed between his eyebrows.

The soldiers had all alighted and were filtering from the platform onto the road where they had begun to form up in a column of threes prior to commencing a march to their barracks. A sergeant bellowed at them to be quiet and the soldiers whispered to each other to shush so as not to antagonise their superior who already looked like he was primed to erupt.

No sign of Johnny. 'You won't miss me,' he said. 'Our eyes will lock onto each other straight away.'

Something must have happened. He had never let her down before. Perhaps he was called away at a moment's notice by his regiment. That was possible, yes. Well then, nothing else for it, she thought. Ask that gentleman for directions. Him with the bowler hat and the big buttons in his black coat. The state of his lady. Done up in her finery. Lovely, she is. Gorgeous.

'I beg your pardon, sir,' she said.

He looked at her and a loose smile played on his lips. She saw mischief in him and did not like it one bit. 'Yes?' he said.

'The Curragh, the military camp, how do I get there?

Though he turned to the lady on his arm he spoke to Rosanna. 'Why – do you want to enlist?'

English, she thought, wouldn't you know it by the smug and snobbish look to his face?

'No. I don't want to soldier; I want a direction.' His face grew concerned. He pointed and she followed his aim and saw that it went to a tall red-brick building, peaked with a crenellated parapet and a Union Jack, stiff in the wind. The camp was comprised of solid buildings spread out in long flanks from the tower about two miles distant across a plain. The rain began to fall in sheets, hard rain carried on a biting wind with no mercy in it. He said, 'You'll find nothing there for yourself. The Provost Marshal or one of his agents will run you. I'm sure of this, if they are at all like the sort I've encountered in Aldershot.'

'I'm looking for Johnny Maguire. He's a sergeant in the 11th dragoons. Where –'

His lady friend looked at her and said, 'Like Mr Tone has just said, you'll find nothing for you in the camp.'

'Go home – here, take this,' he said, holding a pair of tanners in his gloved palm.

'No, thank you; I have a little money.'

'Richard …' his lady said, drawing on his elbow.

They walked away and something went soft in her to see his lady linking him and they chatting to each other under their big black umbrella, his hand steadying it in the face of the wind. Walking out together, like Johnny and she will do.

What in the name of all that's holy could have delayed him? she thought.

CHAPTER 4

RICHARD CUPPED his cousin Josie's elbow and helped her into the trap. The rain ticked against the black hood and fell in large drops from its frilled rim. The car man wore a tall hat and high collar against the elements and his two blinkered horses stood impervious to the challenge of such foul weather.

Richard said, using a grey handkerchief to dry his face, 'That young woman had the clearest blue eyes.'

His cousin frowned and said, 'Fond of waifs, Richard; you're such a sweet.'

'Wasn't she the frailest looking creature, Josie? And her face was ripe with excessive worry – it was like all her plans and hopes had fallen in on her.'

'Perhaps they have, Richard. Mr Lynch! Why the delay?'

A gruff voice thrown over a sodden shoulder, like a throw of earth from a spade, 'For the soldiers to clear the road, Ma'am.'

'Did you see her, Josie, looking up and down the platform?'

'With those blue eyes, Richard – yes, I noticed. Eyes as blue as your own.'

'Straining her neck to look past people in search of her beau.'

Josie sighed, 'And you making yourself overfamiliar, Richard, about to tease her.'

'She was in no mood for it.'

'Not in the least. And who could blame her?'

'I wish she had taken the money.'

'I do so like to help the less well-off, but one could spend a fortune giving money to those in need of it.'

'I wonder if it would be possible to give her a lift?'

Josie said, 'I think not. I have an appointment with Doctor Meade and he does not like to be kept waiting. You always are too keen to help, Richard, and you've done your bit. Besides, the trap would have to be cleaned after her. You may have noticed her eyes, Richard, but evidently not how badly she smelled.'

That evening he presented Josie with a gift of a rosewood tea caddy with inner compartments, decorated with a brass inlay in the shape of acorns and claw feet. Josie was about thirty, a widow whose husband had been killed five years ago in a pistol duel over an unpaid debt, a piffling sum that Richard had at the time advised him to write off. But it was not in Thomas to let a little be lost. He had loved his Rigby duelling pistols and had often quoted advice given by the Provost at Trinity College, '… spend four hours daily at Rigby's pistol gallery.'

At the time Richard had thought rather grimly that Thomas had come up against a man who had spent more time than was recommended in practising and perfecting his shooting skills. A waste of life, Richard thought. Poor Thomas. Poor Josie.

His cousin was a compact little woman, sturdy, always well dressed, well spoken, well intentioned. Excited by his gift, and after praising his exquisite taste, she said, 'I simply must show Mrs Clancy – she's my new cook; she absolutely loves this sort of thing.' He smiled at her. As he moved to the bay window to look out at the street, Josie left the room. He pinched the lace curtain aside, stared out at the hammering rain and sighed hard. He turned and sat in an easy chair, moved it closer to the fireplace. He looked at the red coals, the small blue flames dancing between them and then took in the large room: the oval mirror, the gold-framed paintings of bewigged gentlemen and a barge on a canal. The pale green wall-paper was embossed with claret-coloured Tudor roses; the ceiling had ornate coving and, at the corners, pairs of decorative angels.

This is Josie's *piano nobile*, he thought, and the main storey of her home: the one in which she has invested most of her time, money and energy. We live so well – we close the door on those who live in abject poverty and blind the eye of our conscience to them. Yet perhaps, he thought, it is that blinding that allows us to live with ourselves.

His line of work had seen him visit the home of Edward Hoops in London. This man gathered horse dung from the streets and sold it as fertilizer. He also sold dog turds at a rate of eight pence a bucket to the tanneries for use in the dyeing of leather. Hoops' home was a one-room, overcrowded hovel that smelled of sickness and of dried human and animal waste. For a moment that terrible cloying smell returned to Richard's nostrils. Here, he thought, Josie has someone to take away her cold ash, her waste; to replenish her coal scuttle; to cook her meals; to wash her clothes. And yet, so do I – at night I eat hot food, sip whiskey by the hearth, retire to a warm bed and read by oil lantern. A tug on a cord in my room rings a bell in the pantry and hurries a butler or a maid to my door; all this while Edward Hoops and souls like him scavenge for survival.

Over tea the young woman was strong in his mind. As they'd pulled from the siding she was making her way across the grassland in the direction he had indicated. The advice to go home was better for her than the offer of money, perhaps. In any event she was intent on going her own way. He was sure she was wet through before she'd stepped twenty paces. My cousin is wrong, he thought.

There's always more that one can do.

Chapter 5

JAMES GREANEY rode close to her but the wind and rain –
one a fiddle, the other a bow – muffled his approach. The peaks
of wooded hills to the north-east, long ago a fort for the druids
and Ireland's warrior class, were sheeted in dense cloud. When finally she turned about at the sound of hoof fall and horse snort,
he studied her carefully. She is fierce young to be wandering, he
thought; fourteen, if she's a day.

He said, pushing his voice above the wind, 'Where are you off
to, Miss?'

'The camp.'

'To see your father, is it?'

'No.'

'How old are you, Miss?'

'Eighteen.'

'Indeed, and how old do I look?'

'Thirty.'

'I'm twenty-six.'

So, he thought, I look older than my years and she younger
than hers.

'Well now, 'tis my job, being a Curragh Ranger, to tell you that
you can't go to the camp – only on Thursday, to the market and
then only for an hour.'

'And why amn't I let go? I need to meet someone; he's expecting me.'

'They don't let nightwalkers into the camp, Miss.'

'It's not night yet, sir.'

The truculent lip, he thought; the look about her. Ready to blubber and ready to fight at the same time.

'You know well what I mean. Don't be the smart tongue with me, Miss.'

'I *really* don't know what you mean, sir.'

He sighed and muttered under his breath and his piebald pony seemed to understand this as a prompt because he, too, created a series of noises.

'Go off in that direction there. Ask for Bridget. Tell her James Greaney sent you.'

'That direction – what's there? A house?'

'Jesus, for sure. A fine one, aye; a mansion of a place. Off you go, now.'

She walked on a little until she reached a point where she grew uncertain of where he was sending her and looked back to him for guidance.

He rose and leaned forward in his saddle and jabbed his finger several times at the air. Bleddy thick head on him, she thought, cheeks as red as beetroot and the lump of his Adam's apple like he'd tried to swallow a turnip.

She resumed walking, picturing herself with Johnny, knowing with full certainty that if he were here he'd be holding a big black umbrella over their heads and dripping apologies all over her for being late, explaining the reasons and she pretending to be huffed and keeping it up until he grew a little annoyed with her.

She walked. She coughed. And when she coughed a soreness came to her ribs. No house, she thought... What was that man on about? Oh, there, looking out at me from a smoky furze bush, the eyes wild in her head. Janey …

'Hello …' Rosanna said.

'Hello yourself.'

'That man back there sent me looking for a house and to speak with Bridget. James Greaney, he said his name was.'

'Isn't he the smart bucko for saying that to you – a house indeed?'

'Well …'

'This is the house he's talking about and I'm Bridget Lyons, the mistress of it – for my sins.'

'And you … you live in the bushes?'

'We do. It's a shelter of a poor sort. Have you come to join us, girl?'

'Join?'

'Aye.'

'Can I wait in the bush until the rain blows over?'

Rosanna thought how the woman had a lean, hard look to her. Wrinkles on her face cut like lines she used to draw with a stick in the sands in Bray. Bedraggled hair and her figure sparse, a lick of flesh painted over bone.

And you one to be talking – not a bright pick on you.

There was a hesitancy in Bridget, like she was wondering to herself whether the young one's interests would be best served by her walking on. There was that in her and also another consideration: the young one might own a few coins.

'Come in, come in. You wouldn't keep a duck out in such weather.'

'Thank you.'

Though neither tall nor next it Rosanna had to stoop to the enter the furze bush. The clearing was small inside, the roof a thinly veiled canopy of furze, parts of the grey sky visible, raindrops spitting through. A tarpaulin flapped and Rosanna supposed that the wind had taken it along the roof of furze and that Bridget wasn't of a mood to search for it.

'Move closer to the smoke – 'tis not warm enough to call it a fire.'

God, the state of this home – earth floor, a few sorry chairs, pots and pans. Smell of stew cooking. 'Why didn't you bring a change of clothes?'

'All I had were rags – worse than rags. I left them behind.'

'Jaysus – no one has ever come here as bare as yourself.'

'I won't be bare for too long.'

'Where are you from?'

'Dublin.'

'Do have you a name or is it a secret to you?'

'Rosanna Doyle.'

She gestured Rosanna to a stool whose legs were rooted in the earth. Rosanna moved to it, sat down and held her hands to the fire.

'Have you any money?'

'About three shillings,' Rosanna lied.

'Three … You were counting on meeting a soldier; I'm saying that for sure.'

'If he knew I was enduring this, he would be very cross with himself.'

She caught Bridget giving her a peculiar sidelong look and wondered at the reason.

'I'm sure he would be very cross with himself, Miss Doyle.'

'You might have heard of him: Johnny Maguire. He's a sergeant.'

Bridget rolled her green eyes to the bushy ceiling as though the name was lodged there. When she brought them down she said, 'Aye. Yes … I've heard of him.'

'Really?'

'Yes.'

'A tall, red-haired man – as red-haired as myself?'

'With a nose that burns whenever the least bit of sun gets on it.'

'Yes, that's him!'

'The one and only.'

'Whatever do you mean?'

'I mean nothing girl, nothing at all.'

'We're going to get married.'

Bridget gestured for Rosanna to hand her a ladle. A heavy utensil with '9th Lancers' stamped on its handle. She stirred a pot of
stew – its meaty smell pushed an appetite toward Rosanna.

'I'm delighted for you.'

'How do you know my Johnny?'

'He visits us.'

'Visits here?'

'Visits us is what I said.'

'He brings you food – he's like that, Johnny is, very charitable.'

'Oh, decent to the bone. Now, go back into the furze and find
yourself a dry space, if there is one, and change out of those wet
clothes – here, take this, probably miles too big for you but 'tis
better than what you're wearing.'

'You're very kind.'

'Before you go, a couple of things: don't go near any of the
other girls' stuff and we have a pool for the money we make – to
buy food and things.'

'Here,' she said, handing over a few pence.

'That'll be doing for now.'

'Are the girls at work?'

'Most likely.'

'What is it they do?'

A slow smile broke on Bridget's lips and developed into laughter tinged with irony, cruelty and surprise.

She said, 'Janey Mack but indeed you did come down in the last
shower. Away with you and change …'

Chapter 6

JAMES LOOKED at her, picking her steps through the beads of sheep dirt on the grassy incline till she was gone over the slight rise, her red hair a wisp of sunset. The only glow of the day.

He emptied himself of a sigh then lifted his arse from the saddle and farted. He said to himself, I'd wager there was complete shock in her face when she confronted Bridget and her home of gorse. Her nest. He thought of how this was another poor feck on her way to nothing and less – go pull the nest down, the Head Ranger had told him. He had said he would but his mind was solid that he would do no such thing. Not with the rain hopping off the turf and the wind blowing hard enough to blow a tinker off his missus. The girl was wet through, as though she had just surfaced from a river. And all he could do was send her to a furze bush with its low wall of turves and no roof apart from what the bushes afford. He thought then of how the gold was gone off the furze and the mushrooms scoured from the plains, including the magic ones that the women dried and ground to powder and used as tea or tobacco. With the liquor and tea they often lost the run of themselves and became ferociously violent.

Feck will I go near them, he'd said to himself as he rode across the plains – not a human nor a Christian act would it be. In the back of his mind there was an image of Peggy Smith and how it might not be safe for him to meet with her.

'She'd frighten the lumps out of porridge,' someone had once said of her.

He nudged the piebald forward, the rain falling gently now,

wasting slowly like a bad temper. He was a wirily-built man with short brown hair that was shiny at the pell and finely chiselled features – face gaunt and eyes set close together, engaged somewhat unnaturally with a long beak nose. Sometimes he was of the opinion that his face was comprised of two different ones in keeping, he supposed, with his oul fella's estimation of his nature: 'James, you told that lad one thing and me a differ thing about the same matter.'

His father was cantankerous, brooding and violent when drunk. A person would want nothing to do with himself after listening to him whining off a list of his faults.

'Giddyup there.'

After stabling the piebald in the small yard reserved for those in the civil employ of the military, he went to the Head Ranger's office, lifted the counter's drop leaf and passed through into a room that had a pot-belly stove and iron chimney that rose crooked through the ceiling. The heat shimmered around the stove, lazily dancing.

Kennedy was sitting behind a walnut desk with his spectacles perched above his thick eyebrows, rubbing his eyes, stomach tenting up against his waistcoat. He sighed and lowered his glasses.

'Did ye shift that shower in the lone nest?' he said.

'I did,' James lied.

'There's more over near the edge with Kildare but don't be going near there by yourself.'

'Jaysus no – there'd be nothing of me left if the wrens turned.'

'Nothing is right.'

Kennedy sighed. He had a round, fleshy face with lines either side: frameworks to support those cheeks. He was a shirt and tie man these days and rarely toured the plains. He liked to make out that he had too much paperwork to see to and while he had some, the amount wasn't nearly enough to consume his entire working day. 'I don't know, James,' Kennedy said, tapping a map on his desk with an empty ink bottle.

James moved away from the stove and stood under a painting of a keep on a wooded lake island, the corner torn and hanging like a terrier's tongue. His eyes went to the broken timber slats in the corner of the ceiling where an errant foot had come through during a repair job to the slated roof.

'Sir?'

'I'm due to retire soon.'

James poured water from a plain white jug into a pan and put it on the stove to boil for tea. Best to be direct with this fellow, he thought.

'Have they decided on the new man yet?'

'No, no … Not yet.'

James wanted the job and had spoken of his desire to Kennedy a month ago. Back then there had been a nod from him, a sigh, a pause and then he'd said, 'I'll see what I can do. If I can put in a good word for you.'

This time a longer pause ensued as though he was waiting for James to say a few more words on the matter. When none arrived he moved to the door and looked into the small reception area. He turned about, hands behind his back.

Checking to see if any ears had walked in before he started his tongue: a cute hoor, alright. The bleddy man knows that I'm aware of his pending retirement and he knows I'd like his shoes – why he is acting like a gombeen and starting the works of this news all over?

'Will I be blunt, James?' he said, returning to his chair behind the desk.

'Sure, why not?'

'When my predecessor was here he asked me if I'd like his job and if I did, whether I might like to soften the way for him.'

James moved his eyes to the small sash window and then back to Kennedy.

'He wanted money from you to encourage him to scratch a few lines in your favour, is that so?' James said.

Kennedy showed James his hand, 'Now, I'll tell you this – I was upset at first but then I understood the meanness of the pension and that a little something extra was only fair for him to be getting on with. And seeing as I was to make a little more money myself upon promotion I saw to him and he saw to me and the world didn't stall on its axis.'

James felt a surge of anger. Bad cess to that lad, he thought. He had always understood that the position of Head Ranger was his when Kennedy retired. It was a tradition for the job to be handed on to the Deputy Ranger. His predicament made quick inroads into him – Kennedy could write bad lines or no lines which was the same thing. His superiors could easily act on Kennedy's recommendation and decide to give the job to someone else.

Kennedy said, with a smile like a nameplate on a coffin, 'You have to be well got to get what you want.'

James remained silent.

'Would that work for you, James, to see someone else wear your shoes?'

'How much more to soften the way?'

James thought that he would simply have to press the wrens a little harder for coins, tell them it was in their interest to have him made up as boss and not some jennet who didn't care a toss for their plight. He cared – they knew it – and he didn't know why he did but it was a fact about himself that he could as soon do without.

'We'll discuss it over tea,' Kennedy said.

Chapter 7

LORD PRESERVE me …

The shivers were in her and she wasn't sure if the blame for it lay in the shock of being in the bush or the absence of her Johnny or if her very soul had suddenly abandoned her.

A dry space, a floor of earth, a perfume of furze. A dress too wide and long for her but blue, her favourite colour – the colour of bluebells with a hem of wild garlic. The perishing wind seemed to pare at her very bones. Her teeth chattered. She imagined that they would land at her feet if they beat off each other with even a little more force. Is this what I have come to? she asked herself, taking in the bed of musty hay. She prayed silently for Johnny to come and mend things for her. She believed that he would be vexed when he learned that she had whiled away time in a furze bush with the smoke cutting at her lungs and her eyes. She recalled seeing Johnny in his best uniform when they'd met that first time in the park. He had such a lovely smile. He liked to talk. He was polite and made her feel special. After telling her she was the prettiest-looking girl in the whole of Dublin, he added, 'We'll have to celebrate your birthday … we must.'

They went out for dinner a few days later and drank wine and afterwards they walked with no particular destination in mind. The night was balmy, rich with stars. They started to kiss near a woods and in with the trees they kissed some more and then lay down on the ground, he having put his jacket down to save her from the dew. When she stopped his hand from venturing too far down, he sat up and she could tell he was annoyed with her. But she believed him when he said he wasn't put out. At least not with her. He was, he said, soon to be leaving with the dragoons for the Curragh and he did not want to go anywhere without her. She was sad at the pending loss of him and merry from the wine. Dizzy and giddy by turn. And she did not want to end the night like this. So she let his hand wander and let him do what he wanted because it was what she wanted too. It felt right. Though he had hurt her a little, that first time …

'You'll be grand,' he said, ''tis only a drop of blood – you'll be getting to like the jaunting later. You'll see.'

'How is it you know, Johnny?'

'My head is never out of a book,' he said, listing off a few titles. The things he knows, Johnny.

'Be sure to follow me down – I don't want to be missing you.'

'Where will I stay?'

'You let me worry about that; you won't be disappointed.'

There was strength of meaning in his words. Steel – yes, steel …

CHAPTER 8

THE PRIEST lived in an ivy-covered house down a laneway off the main street. It was a wide street with conventional buildings on one side only, the other holding a cavalry barracks, and ending at a bridge that crossed the River Liffey. Straw had been spread on the street to lessen the noise of iron-shod wheels: a sign that someone was ill or dying and quiet was needed and thus paid for. Josie had arranged the interview. She was a member of the Parish Committee and helped dispense cakes and teas on social occasions. Richard had been ill this morning with his stomach but felt well enough in the afternoon to walk the short distance from his cousin's home to meet with Father Charles Taylor. His housekeeper, Mrs Dobbyn, was a stubby little woman who wasn't the least bit friendly and gave the regard that his knock was an unnecessary disruption to her daily routine. His greeting was not returned. She invited him with a pointed finger to hang his hat and coat on an antlered stand in the hall and with the same finger showed him the door to the living-room, a genial room of green walls and green quilted sofas and easy chairs.

Father Taylor turned from the tall bay window and smiled. Richard thought that his smile was like that of a sun on a frosty morning, without heat enough to burn off the frost that stared out from the shade. 'Sit, please,' Father Taylor said.

He was a gangly man of about forty and his face had a greyish pallor that fell just short of matching the grey of his eyes. Richard could not discern much about the man by reading his face, other than what was immediately noticeable. He had heavily knitted eyebrows and the veins in his cheeks were as though they had been traced there by the tip of a red hot-poker. Father Charles Taylor was a man with laboured breathing and it stirred the hairs growing from his nostrils.

The priest put a hand to the small of his back as he lowered himself into the easy chair opposite Richard. He removed a cushion and threw it onto the sofa.

'My back aches from the hunt – a slight tumble,' he said.

'I'm sorry to hear about your discomfort.'

'Yes, well,' he waved a hand, the back of which had veins as thick as roots. 'I'll be fine, God willing. So, Mr Dickens wants you to write an article about the nightwalkers?'

'Yes.'

'A most prolific author, I must say. I did so enjoy his Pickwick –'

'He is indeed prolific.'

'And a prolific father as well, into the bargain,' Father Taylor chuckled

'Given your knowledge of Mr Dickens' work, you'll understand why such a story as the plight of the poor unfortunates on the Curragh would appeal to him. They do live in atrocious conditions, you'll agree.'

'It's their choice – they have the workhouse in Naas that offers them food and shelter. They're bad women, Mr Tone, bad women. And a whip is what some of them – not all of them, mind – deserve and well deserve.'

He had not liked the man in the first instance and there was to be no change in this regard after that remark.

'Who decides which of them is good?'

'Decides?'

No give in his face. No self-deprecating smile; no tease. A man full of the seriousness of himself and his beliefs.

Richard said, 'They're called the wren women.'

'They are and worse. The vilest creatures God ever set two feet to: drunken whores that not even Babylon herself would have been depraved enough to house.'

'They are living in dire and atrocious conditions.'

Father Taylor leaned forward, his expression changing: the drawing out of a tide to reveal a shore of seaweed and dead things. He said, 'Let me tell you something, sir: the hospital on the Curragh camp last year recorded 589 cases of venereal disease amongst the troops, a devil's blight visited upon them by your so-called Curragh wrens.'

'Of the women, how many cases?'

'I don't know. Does it matter – would your *Gazette* readers be interested in women who spurn the efforts made by decent people to help them?'

'Are there other ways in which they can be helped?'

'There is ample enough being done for them.'

'Is there not more than one *ought* to do?'

'Have you met with these creatures?'

'It appears to me to that whilst the soldiers receive treatment for their conditions, the women with whom they consort receive absolutely none.'

'I ask you again, Sir, have you met with these dregs?'

'Not yet.'

'When you do, you'll see exactly what I mean. Perhaps it would have served this interview better if you had first spoken to them. You would have come here better prepared to understand my point of view.

'I see.'

'I'm very much afraid, Sir, that you do not see.'

Swords were drawn, Richard understood.

'Can you tell me why a mere twelve pounds was spent in one

year on medicines for the prostitutes in the Naas workhouse, when wages for the chaplains amounted to forty pounds? Is this not a –'

The priest rose to his feet and said, 'I think it's high time that you and your insolence were on your way.' He shouted for Mrs Dobbyn – twice – and when she appeared he said for her to show his guest to the door. During the time it took for her to arrive the priest remained silent and Richard had no inclination to intrude upon this silence.

CHAPTER 9

ROSANNA WENT into the main living area after changing and spoke with Bridget, feeling dry and lost in oversized clothes. Tired, too. Evening was closing in, darkness encroaching. It had stopped raining. Bridget sipped from a bottle of whiskey she'd taken from under a pile of clothing in what she called her space, a little crawl way into the tightly knotted bones of furze off the main floor. She offered the bottle to Rosanna who shook her head.

'Tell no one about the bottle – the lack of that substance turns me wicked. Do you understand me, lass? And you'd want a trough of the stuff to keep the Peggy one.'

'I won't say a word.'

Rosanna basked in the warmth of the turf and stick fire, loving the soft glow of it on her face. 'Throw sticks on that fire like a good woman – they won't land there by themselves.'

Rosanna stirred her hand to a neat stack of turf and sticks.

'When you've done that stir that oul ladle in the pot.'

Rosanna did this, half-tempted to bring the spoon to her lips.

'Don't even dream of it, girl – there's hardly enough for the pair of mouths that's expecting it. If there's anything left over you can have it.'

Bridget sighed and dropped to her hunkers to a battered biscuit tin. She opened the lid and surfaced stubs of candle and two lanterns.

'Light them wicks and stick them in the glass pieces.'

'Okay.'

'It's aisy see that you're a woman used to doing what she's told.'

'I like to help.'

'Good.'

Rosanna felt the itch rise in her lungs. She began to cough.

'Jaysus, that's a rasp and a half,' Bridget said.

'Ah, it comes and goes.'

'Like a man.'

'Not all men.'

'If you say so.'

'Where do I …? I need to… you know …'

'No chamber-pot here, lass – we had one but one of the girls from a nest thought she had more of a need than us of it – thieving bitch, God be good to her. We must be getting another. A pot that is, not a thief – we've enough of those as it is.'

'So …'

'You can empty yourself in a bucket outside or go to the nearest furze to us, that'd be out the opening to your left – do be minding your step for there's sheep shite and fox shite and human shite and one foot in any and you'll be sleeping in the rough tonight, for you will not get back in here and that's the God's honest truth.'

'Okay.'

'Bring a wad of grass with you – there look, or a slab of moss. There, that's it.'

Rosanna carried a lantern and made to leave.

'Rosanna?'

'Yes?'

'Fox is worst of all.'

'I'll be careful.'

'Watch out for the skullers.'

'Skullers?'

'Men who wait in the furze to grab a hauld of you when you're in a delicate way. And if they come near you, don't scream; you may just put up with what you're getting. They'll skull you first so you mightn't feel a thing they do to you, if you're lucky.'

'I'll scream, I will,' Rosanna said breathlessly.

'If you think you'll fight, bring a knife – none of us go there without a knife.'

Bridget wiped a blade in her apron and proffered the knife to Rosanna by the handle.

'Now, girl, use it or it'll be used on you.'

'Oh, God.'

'What's that, glinting round your neck?'

Rosanna knew immediately and was angry with herself for her carelessness.

'Show us.'

'Oh that – that's my mother's. It never comes off.'

Bridget inched closer, squinting, ''Tis nice, very nice. What's it hold?'

'A picture of my mother.'

'Open it. 'Tis gold, is it? Let me feel it.'

Before Rosanna could answer, Bridget held up the locket; the chain bit into Rosanna's flesh, such was the force of the tug.

Bridget, using a thumbnail, slid aside the lid and squinted hard at the small portrait.

'Give me more light,' she said.

Rosanna raised the lantern.

'Jaysus, 'tis like looking at yourself. 'Tis even a bit like me in my best days. By the blazes …'

She closed the locket and eased it against Rosanna's breastbone. Her finger came up like a sword, 'Let no one see it or it'll be gone on you, have no doubt about it. Gone. Good gold it is. Old gold.'

'I won't.'

'Off you go before you burst all over my clean floor.'

She laughed and Rosanna read into it all sorts of things: humour, despair, sarcasm and threat. She was a woman full of warnings. As

Rosanna walked to the furze, she buttoned herself up to the neck. It was cold. The lantern threw a shadow of herself onto the grass. Apart from the paltry light the world was completely black. A lost soul with only a tiny flame to keep her from being at one with the night.

CHAPTER 10

IN FROM her toiletry, Rosanna lingered at the fire and then bid goodnight to Bridget who hadn't been very talkative since Rosanna's return and appeared slightly on edge. Like she were the wife of a brute who was soon to come home to her and create ructions for no reason or any reason.

Rosanna started coughing: God, it tears at my lungs so, she thought, like a sharp scissors to a ribbon.

'Jaysus, you'll be no good on your back, that's for sure. Weak as a kitten, neither shape nor make to you. There's more meat to be found on a tinker's stick after he flaying his donkey.'

'I'm fine,' Rosanna said, "tis only the effect of the day.'

'Fine! I'd believe it out of a corpse's mouth before yours.'

'I just need a night's sleep.'

'Aye.'

'Goodnight again, so.'

'Goodnight to you, young one. Will you be able to sleep on an empty belly?'

'I –'

'Here, go and take a couple of mouthfuls of the stew and a bit of that black bread there. Take it with you – it's probably best that you're not in sight when the others come.'

'Perhaps I should stay to meet them.'

'Tomorrow is soon enough.'

'They might think it rude of me.'

'Rude, you say? Will you hurry and take your sups and go close your eyes.'

Rosanna heard the ruckus then of drunken women talking and arguing, rising above the bleating of disturbed sheep. She sipped once and again from the stew, dipped her bread in it and brought it with her to her bed of dank hay.

'Mind the rats,' said the woman of warnings.

From her bed Rosanna heard the chatter ebb to silence, the flap of tarpaulin pulled aside like a loud rip of stitching in a garment.

'How ye?' Bridget said.

No answer.

'Back from your courting,' Bridget said. 'Did ye think to bring me a little something for my chest? Well, Peggy?'

'I did not.'

As the women continued to talk, Rosanna could put names to the voices.

'What ails that chest of yours anyhow?' Peggy said, her voice cold and rough.

'The cold, Peggy.'

'The could.' A shrill voice – Violet.

'The could, as Scobie says, the oul bastard,' Peggy said.

'Oh, we're in the wit tonight, girls,' Bridget said.

'We'd a great oul time of it in the tavern, we had, didn't we Peggy? ' Violet said.

Bridget said, 'In the tavern? The Scobie lad let youse in?'

'He did so out of fear of what might be done to him if he opened his trap,' Peggy said.

Violet said, 'You'd be sick of the rain, so you would.'

Always, Bridget thought, poor Violet tries to steer your woman off the course of what might ignite or, as is often the case, reignite her temper.

Violet said, 'I'm starved, I am.'

Bridget said, 'How did ye get on?'

'Middling,' Violet replied. 'Only middling.'

Not much for the common purse, Bridget thought.

She said, 'We've a guest.'

Violet was quickest to respond, 'Have we? Who?'

Peggy said, 'There's enough work for eight more of us – I'll have to be cutting myself in two to keep the rabbits happy.'

'She's a wee thing with a bad cough and a yarn about a soldier boy who she said wants to marry her.'

The pair erupted in laughter.

Peggy said, 'Jaysus love her.'

Violet said, 'Here's a bottle for you, Bridget.'

'A bottle? You're very good, Violet. Now, Peggy, don't go disturbing your woman – she's out for the count.'

'I will if I want to, Bridget – you're nothing only a passenger here. A wizened up oul yoke that no man wants to saddle and –'

Violet cut in, 'Peggy, now.'

'It's true, so it is and don't be going saying that it's not.'

'She does our cooking and our washing and other little things.'

Bridget railed, 'You're a hurtful woman, Peggy; a wicked one with a wicked temper but while you might best others here and around, you'll not best me – there's no man would want you either after I'd be finished with you.'

Violet said, 'That stew smells nice, Bridget – can I have some?'

Peggy snuffled contemptuously and said, 'I want some too, with a fair bit of meat in it.'

'I've a hand on the ladle,' Bridget said in a hard way, beating its basin against the rim.

Chapter 11

ROSANNA HAD stolen in under the blankets fully dressed yet could not find the cosy warmth she had hoped for. She chewed on the bread that the stew hadn't softened by much and her mind whispered its thoughts, so afraid was she of the change in atmosphere in the nest brought about by the arrival of the others, especially Peggy.

A scuttling noise. Rats. Each segment of her spine froze over in turn.

It's only for one night, she told herself; tomorrow night I'll be in a warm bed after having a decent supper. Definitely no clothes under the blankets tomorrow, not with Johnny beside me to keep me snug and warm and safe. That's if I don't fetch my end here.

She swallowed the last of the bread and rubbed the small rise of her belly, touched her locket, breathed a small prayer, watched the vapour of the Hail Mary evaporate …

She had never heard people eating the way they did. They slurped and chewed hard. She was still hungry but would not show her face to them out of fear. Peggy spoke like her temper lurked just beneath the surface of her tongue, ready to lash out. The smell of drink was much stronger than the smell of stew. One of the women belched hard. Peggy complained about a soldier who had lain with her, he enjoying himself no end when he said he had no money till pay day and would she mind waiting till then, and he'd pay her her dues. She bit his ear and told him to be away with himself.

Violet carried on in the same vein and said the same lad had tried that with her and she'd put him out, too. Bridget sighed and said she'd been taken along that road a long while ago with a lad and the next thing she heard wasn't he on the troop train off to fight in India. Word got to her later that he'd lost his two legs in a rock slide at the Khyber Pass. Served him right, Peggy said. Violet said losing two legs was bad luck. Bridget said nothing. Then the itch came at Rosanna's lungs and she coughed and couldn't stop. She fought to control it and managed to, easing phlegm on to the hay. Like old man's drool in a lunatic asylum. Silence then, complete were it not for the lonely bleat of a distant sheep.

Peggy said, 'Bridget, she's a ruin! A ruin isn't what we need.'

'She'll beg; by God, if she doesn't wring a coin from a miser's pocket my name's not Bridget Lyons.'

'A coin! If she's going to stay she'll need to be doing more than beg. One idle woman is enough to be supporting.'

Rosanna shook her head violently.

No! her mind screamed. No!

She had only known Johnny in that way. She used to see the prostitutes in Dublin. They were all hard and coarse women, painted up so as not to look so. Beg? Me? she thought. Johnny, for their sakes, would not want to hear what they were saying. Especially after he learned that she was having his baby. He would shut them up. Peggy, too. She was sure the baby would be a boy and had already made up her mind to call him Samuel after her father, although if Johnny didn't like the name she would not go against him.

'Hurry,' she whispered, 'Johnny, wherever you are, hurry here.'

He was, she was convinced, worried out of his mind not knowing where she was, if she had let him down by not coming.

Chapter 12

'CLOSE THE door, James; we have a matter to discuss,' Kennedy said.

The bastard, James thought. He wants more money. I gave him all I had yesterday and this afternoon he's back for another fill. Every shilling I had, he got. I even threw in the long earrings that Bridget gave me to sell for her.

Kennedy had the mock face of a widow pretending to be sorrowful at her husband's grave. James saw this in him and thought how like the widow Molloy he resembled, a woman observed doing a little jig outside the graveyard gates during the moments her mask slipped. His father insisted that the woman was beside herself with grief and that everyone dealt with sorrow in her own way. The oul lad always was soft on Catherine Molloy.

James kept his face straight and unconcerned though his insides were astir with a sense of dread. Had any of the wrens spoke up? Said how he was taking money from them, acting as their agent for the pawn shop in Naas? If it arose, James fixed it in his mind to laugh off the allegation of corruption. After all, it was his word against theirs. If they had spoken out of place he would deal with them later. They might not have said anything about him, for he had never been unkind to them and did not tax them much – sometimes not at all.

Kennedy looked at James and looked away to the pot-belly stove, wisps of smoke rising from under its lid.

'There's no easy way of saying this, James,' Kennedy said.

'Errah, try using your mouth; it's a help.'

Kennedy's eyes went smaller than their usual smallness.

'I received a letter this morning, James, from our superiors.'

'I see.'

Kennedy sighed and held his hands in the air as though he were holding up an invisible weight.

'Tell me, so, and be done with it – I didn't get the job, is that it? Who's the new fella?'

'You didn't get the job … yet. I applied in poor faith for an extension to my contract and they've granted me six months as a sign of appreciation for my endeavours. It was, I won't lie to you, a great and welcome surprise.'

James said nothing. He felt his lips tighten.

'This means what?' he said.

'A delay for you is all. No more than that.'

'The money and things I gave you?'

'What of them? It's a deposit, James; you're young – you have many years ahead of you in this position.'

'A deposit? I gave you the sum agreed and we sealed a deal yesterday, did we not? We shook hands on it.'

Kennedy tapped his index finger on the letter and said, 'I have the impression from reading this letter, James, that a further six months is there for me if I request it, perhaps a year – do you want to wait that long?'

He has me in a bind. Bastard.

James nodded, chewed on his lower lip. In an instant Kennedy was a flurry of energy, his voice changing, lifting, not low as it had been, as though it had been that way to converse with a snake. Snake to snake, James thought.

'The Provost Marshall has lent us some men and I've been over to speak with Cosgrove, the relief officer – we're going to move the wrens off the Gibbet Rath …'

'When?'

'Now, James – right now. The women have a soldier spy and he seems well able to tell them whenever we've a move planned.'

'I doubt that.'

' Have no doubts.'

'I –'

Kennedy rose from his chair, leaned his hands on the edge of his desk, 'We shall see this morning, James. Let's go.'

What can I do, only go along with it? he thought as he nursed his piebald behind the small column of mounted troop, only go along with it. At least I don't know these women too well. These are new nests we're heading to at the Gibbet Rath, a great old fort where they used hang the highwaymen and, in '98, did slaughter the rebels from Kildare. 350 souls, they say.

They rode the north road from camp, cantering across the plains, through a deep dyke in the rath, across its flat space, exiting at a deeper dyke. He smelled the fires from the encampment: outdoor fires, now that the rain had cleared. The acrid stench of burning sticks clung to clothes and skin like no other type of smoke, reminding him of tinker camps he had often passed by when he was a child.

He remained on his pony as the troop dismounted and dragged the women and children from their nests, breaking up what little they owned and setting fire to their shelters. He watched the flames take hold, the fire raging grey and orange and soon, he knew, all that'd remain would be a skeletal frame of blackened gorse, the floor covered with dirty soot that'd burn the paws of dogs and other creatures who meandered through it.

Kennedy sat perched on his saddle. Fat man with his spectacles, not a giblet of compassion in him. Impassive as a rock, he is. James asked himself if this was what he really wanted to do with his life: to assist with the burning of all that belonged to wretched people like these? He tried to shut his ears to the banshee wailing of the women and children, to the effect it must be having on some of the troops because, truth be known, they were throwing out their own.

They shouted, 'Where'll we go? What'll we do?'

Kennedy stared sidelong at James, for it was he whom the women addressed.

'The workhouse,' James said with a flourish of his hand, so quickly done it was like the flash of a whip without the accompanying crack of air. 'Where else?'

'Ah James!'

The women, he knew, rejected the workhouse in Naas because they said it was worse than living on the Curragh. They said priests lectured you and no drink was allowed and you were locked up and told what to do – better to die a free bird than one looking out between the ribs of a cage. And besides, they were accommodated in lean-to shelters outside the workhouse, not even considered good enough citizens to be classed with the classless.

Kennedy said, 'You're popular, so it seems.'

'I see no sign of Cosgrove with his transportation – the women are supposed to be provided with –'

Kennedy said, 'I know what they're supposed to be provided with, James. But the walk will do them good …'

He turned then and set off for his office, taking the shortest route.

James watched the fire spread to gorse that hadn't been lived in. How one thing leads to another, he thought. A spark, then another, then a blaze.

Chapter 13

THE FOLLOWING evening in the nest, the Curragh darkness shut out, the grassland's voices lingered outside. A dog barked; the diminishing beat of horse hooves, the wind's fingers on the branches. That morning Bridget had told Rosanna that the soldiers were away on manoeuvres for a few days. Rosanna considered her options. If she was not allowed to enter the camp, she could not contact Johnny. Her money would not last very long if she took lodgings in town. Bridget knew Johnny and she'd said she would get word to him about his visitor. So Rosanna resolved to see how the day went before making a decision. What Bridget had said troubled her deeply. How many days did she consider a few? To take her mind off things she had busied herself. She washed her clothes in an aluminium tub, wrung them by hand and draped them to dry over a furze bush. She gathered armloads of kindling, held a dock leaf to her shin to heal a nettle sting, looked all around her at the flat landscape, not liking the fact that the wind seemed to have no sense of direction. She stared at the distant hills to the north-west, the far-off mountains to the east, at the passing civilian horse traffic, the countless plumes of smokes that billowed from the camp's chimneys. She'd stayed out of the furze house to avoid meeting with Peggy and was glad when she returned to have the place to herself. In the middle of the afternoon it began to rain and so caught up was she worrying about Johnny that she forgot to take in her clothes off the bush. On her way back from wherever she was, Bridget brought them in for her and said she was to take the sheep shite out of her eyes 'and look lively'.

The day done, the women sat in silence around the small fire, staring into the reddish orange furnace, the kettle resting close by, losing the steam of itself. Fire-washed faces, the heat a comfort, coaxing them to drowsiness, an anaesthetic to their cares. Not a complete shutting out of these, however; they were as present as the noises of the plains. Smell of drying clothes on the backs of their wearers.

Infrequently the outside noises encroached earnestly in the wind's show of its hand against the hessian door, the fabric draped across the top of a strip of corrugated iron pushing in, sackcloth gloving the hand of the wind; and then this effort would fall away and depart, whistling on its way to places more easily accessible. Violet had just spoken and each of the others had listened to what she'd had to say: Rosanna out of respect and the others because their companion was not one who ordinarily had much to say for herself, and so they gave their ears easier than what might otherwise have been the case if she'd been the talkative sort.

'A matter of honour,' Peggy said quietly.

'Yes,' Violet breathed, 'imagine. Fighting over me.'

Sticks crackled and fell in on the core of the fire. A splash of sparks quickly died to darkness. 'Over you?' Peggy replied, 'Imagine.' And she said again, 'A matter of honour.'

Bridget rubbed her calf where veins ached. She noticed that young Rosanna was sitting among them and yet wasn't within a bull's bellow of the nest. Away with the fairies. 'That Johnny lad is some fairy, all right,' she muttered.

Peggy nudged Rosanna in the ribs, 'What do you say?'

Rosanna said, 'About what?'

'Are you deaf as well as stupid? Soldiers fighting over your wan there, with her scraggly brown hair and no chin and small chest.'

'She is very pretty.'

Violet was skinny with a lovely oval face and her fair hair

47

smelled of shampoo and faintly of beer. Her hair was tied in a pony-tail with a strip of dark cloth.

'Prettier than me, do you think?'

'You're pretty too,' Rosanna said, airing the truth but not saying what was in her to say, which was that Peggy wasn't as pretty as Violet nor half as friendly.

Bridget said, 'What's pretty got to do with it? I thought it was about honour.'

Peggy said, 'Yes. Fecking honour. You're so right – tell us all about the honour thing, Violet.'

Shadows of their souls played on the walls of mud and furze, walls that melted under heavy rain; walls that gave out smells of damp earth and decaying brush, trapped whispers, lost dreams, living nightmares, all fogged with the cloud of smoke and rinse of alcohol. 'Guess what it was about?' Violet teased.

'Guess my behind,' Peggy said on a heavy snort.

'Yes, one guess each,' Bridget said, 'I do so love a game.'

'You first, then,' Peggy said.

'Okay. Violet – both want to marry you, to take you away from here?'

'That's two fecking guesses!' Peggy said, shaking her thick, dark mane.

Violet said quietly, 'No.'

'Ah that's a pity,' Rosanna said, 'I was hoping it would be something like that.'

'You're next, Rosanna,' Peggy said.

'They're fighting to see which one will be your beau.'

'Chief beau of all the beaus,' Peggy said, bottom lip dripping with sarcasm.

The wind rose again, like a creature that had been asleep and was suddenly roused by a taste of danger or of something else strange that was afoot.

'Sorry, Rosanna; you're wrong,' Violet said, shaking her head, drawing her lips tightly closed.

Peggy leaned forward on her upturned pail and cracked her knuckles and released a fart. Then another.

'There's an awful wind in me,' she said.

'Still? After that release?' Bridget said, cupping her hand to her nose.

'The stink!' Violet said.

'Rosanna, pull aside the sack and let some air in,' Bridget said.

Rosanna reached out a hand and whished the sackcloth aside. A hard breeze danced in and circled about and kissed the fire with a heavy breath, raising sparks of alarm.

'Close it, for the love of God; the wind is darting up me hole,' Peggy said.

Rosanna stood to rearrange the cloth door. The blast of cold air had touched her to the very marrow. She felt something give inside her – her child catching a chill?

'Peggy?' Bridget said.

'I would say it's over one lad getting it for free and the other having to pay for it, and the lad paying for it is sore after discovering the fact.' She clapped her hands together.

Violet said, 'Near enough, but not spot on.'

'Tell us,' Bridget said.

'I did charge one more than the other and when Rodney asked why he had to pay more I said the truth to him: it was harder to take him into me than William.'

'William is easier work all right,' Peggy nodded.

'How so?' Rosanna queried.

'Because Rodney has a huge prick that's too big for comfort,' Peggy said.

'An awful yoke of a thing altogether,' Bridget agreed.

'It's about size, so, not honour,' Peggy said.

'Aye,' Bridget said on the back of a loud sigh.

'The two started jeering each other in the billets,' Violet said. 'It got right out of hand, they went at each other with bayonets.'

Rosanna said, 'That's terrible.'

'Nothing terrible to it,' Peggy said. 'When is the fight?'

'Tomorrow in Donnelly's hollow.'

Bridget said, 'Rosanna, Donnelly bate the living dirt out of two English champions in the hollow some fifty years ago. Me mother – God be good to her – used to tell me she and her father had seen him hammer Cooper. A long arm, he had, Donnelly.'

'Longer than Rodney's old mick?' Peggy said with a strong rise of coarse laughter.

Bridget said, 'Down below his knees his hands used hang.'

'That place is used for ructions other than for fighting,' Peggy said, her forefinger parallel to her nose, 'I'll say no more.'

'What time is the fight?' Bridget asked.

'During lunch, so the officers won't be about.'

'We'll go see it,' Peggy said.

'Aye, I do so like to see a good fight,' Bridget said.

Rosanna wondered if Johnny would be there. More than likely not: he had to be away somewhere or he would be with her. It would be best to check as he must be at a loss, searching for and worrying about her.

A windy day, the sun appearing in fits and starts, the grass worn in the centre of the hollow. The steep embankments overlooking the clearing were crowded with soldiers in their red tunics and white breeches, some smoking clay pipes, others offering and accepting wagers. Rosanna strained her eyes but did not see Johnny. 'Ah, he must be away on duty,' she said to herself, her eyes returning to the spectacle of the two bare-chested men squaring up to each other in the little ring. Shouts and cheers rose from the gallery of spectators. A horse, startled by the sudden burst of noise, reared its head and whinnied. A lot of wrens were present, women from the other nests on the Curragh whom the others knew and with whom they exchanged greetings and banter.

'I hope the long lad loses,' said one woman.

'You call him long?' Peggy said. 'You don't know what long is.'

The seconds stood back and the battle commenced. Arms bent at the elbows, fists clenched and raised like two clubs with ridges of thick knuckles as on a blackthorn stick, the men closed in on each other. Both soldiers were tall and broad and wore neat and groomed moustaches. Handsome men. The loathing each had for the other revealed in his steady unflinching stare and insulting expression.

Bridget tugged on Rosanna's elbow and pulled her along in pursuit of the others who were hurrying to get a closer look.

Cheers and jeers of equal measure. Rosanna stared, drinking the scene, her veins beginning to bubble with excitement. Violet was on her toes crying for Rodney and then William, no clear favourite for her affections.

It was Rodney who scored first, his fist landing a punch to William's jaw, dispatching an eye-tooth that fell at Rosanna's feet. She stepped back and looked at the shiny piece of bloodstained ivory. 'Look!' Violet said. 'Good on you, Rodney!'

William, fired up by the loss of his tooth, recovered his composure. He pummelled his fists into Rodney's ribs. The sound of breaking bone, the anguished cry and the disconsolate roar and sighing of the crowd as realisation seeped in that Rodney was beaten. Hardly a contest at all.

Peggy roared at Rodney and insulted him, his mother and his father. 'Get up, ye no good feck! Me money is riding on you!'

Violet remained silent: she was busily sewing William deeper into her affections.

Bridget said, 'It wasn't worth bothering my arse to come see.'

Rosanna's eyes were wide and staring, not at the tooth nor the victor nor the vanquished nor the crowd milling around them but at Johnny on the opposite embankment.

'It is him!' she said.

Her heartbeat quickened; her stomach got the butterflies.

A glimpse of him was all, but it was enough for her to start herself into action and hurry after him. The jostling crowd delayed her progress and their shouts and loud talk buried her calls to him. When she peaked the far side she saw many pockets of red-jacketed soldiers before her, all heading in small groups to the camp. She could not discern him from the others. A sense of loss and disappointment in her; her throat ached.

At least he is about; he isn't away, she thought.

She felt a great load go from her. Like the push of the wind against her soul had taken itself away. And yet some questions began to pierce through her excitement: If he is about, why isn't he enquiring after me? Does he think I am still in Dublin? Did he not receive my letter?

Chapter 14

RICHARD DECLINED to accept an offer of a trap to the plains. It was a sunny morning not far off noon and he wanted to walk off a late breakfast that was not sitting well in his stomach.

'You're sure, Richard?' Josie said. 'It's no trouble for Mr Lynch to bring you.'

'I am. The well-being of my constitution has put this demand on me.'

He smiled.

'Less of your strong brandy and potent cigars might benefit it more – and thinking before you speak,' she said with gentle reproach.

He walked along the main street, going east out of town. Not a cloud to be seen and the distant mountains the clearest he'd seen them in the days he had been here. He was glad of the blackthorn cane that Josie insisted he take, not to aid his step, she said, but to ward off bad-tempered dogs he might encounter. It has a dual purpose, so, he'd said, to propel and to deter.

His writings were coming along well and he was sure that Charles would be well pleased. As an editor Charles was strict and demanding; Richard had learned a lot from him. His books and his reputation made for a good ice-breaker at dinners and tea parties. All wanted to know of the man; it was as if they took it for granted that Richard knew all of what there was to know about him. Or at least the important pieces worth knowing.

Josie was less hostile to him this morning. Although she had not said so, he was aware that Father Taylor had mentioned their meeting to her and hadn't spoken too kindly of him – indeed, had probably reproached her for having foisted such a scurrilous pressman upon him.

But hard words mellow over time and she'd softened. For a day he had contemplated moving into lodgings but held off on this action as this probably would have widened the schism beyond repair.

Family, he said to himself.

At the edge of the plain he stopped to look at the green acres: treeless, coated with islands of furze and flocks of sheep. A troop of cavalry at a slow trot bringing cannon somewhere. He crossed the road and began to cut in across the plain, along a trail in the grass – a trace of ancientness, he was certain – walking the bones of it: the impression of a road that people walked two or three thousand years ago, coming at us like the past always seems to do. He angled himself in the direction of a clump of furze that had puffs of smoke rising from it. Not so distant, he thought.

Drawing closer he saw that the fire was tiny, a few embers of furze sticks on the burn. Under the lee side of the bushes he noted a store of pots and pans. Blankets and clothing draped across part of the bushes where the sun bore down the most.

He saw her emerge from the bush, half-stooped. She fixed a strip of canvas to the side by hooking a noose of rope over a branch.

'Stay in place this time,' she said to the clothes.

When she turned she noticed him and her eyes filled with fire that quickly gave way to a sheen of meekness. He understood her in that instant. She was as Mr Lynch had described, 'A right cute hoor.'

She would not dare enter a fight that she knew she had no hope of winning.

She said, 'The name's Bridget. And, well, fine sir, 'tis no one here for you only meself.'

54

She laughed to indicate that she understood he wouldn't be wanting her and would not be hurt by rejection.

'Ah, not today, thanks. It's a different sort of business call. I'm a press man and I've been commissioned to write a piece about your good selves – I'd be most pleased if you would speak with me… My name is Richard Tone.'

'I thought you were come to warn us off the Curragh.'

'No … no.'

'And why would you want to write about us?'

'To make people aware of the conditions that you live in.'

Bridget scoffed and shook her head, 'And what good will that do for us or you?'

'I'll be paid for writing the article and it might help to improve matters for you. Publicity can help stir consciences; public outrage is the scourge of politicians.'

'I see. And will I be paid for talking to you?'

'A little, I suppose.'

'I've never been paid for talking; to get a little money for doing so would be a pleasure. Come on so, we'll step inside. Mind your head off the briars.'

He followed her inside and found he couldn't straighten to his full height. His eyes swept around, noticing that the living quarters, such as they were, extended further back and to the wings of the main area. A lair not too dissimilar to those of wild beasts.

'Not the driest nor the best of palaces you've sat yourself down in,' she said, nodding for him to take to a legless easy chair, one of three circling a fire set with kindling and turf.

'You can have yourself a fancy bath tonight so don't be worrying about the biteen of dirt and the starved fleas; you'll be grand.'

He knew his expression had given him away and said, 'You're right, Bridget, of course.'

He sat down.

'I'd offer you a drop of tae but we're out – I'm not long after packing young Rosanna off to town to buy some; she might be back with it before you go.'

He felt the back of the chair give way when he leaned backwards and immediately righted himself.

'Nothing here is in the best of condition,' she said.

'One can't expect it to be otherwise – and I can live without tea. I've brought you a small something for the Curragh chill.'

He reached in his pocket and showed her the bottle.

'Rum; ah, you're a kind heart. I'll talk to your good self for nothing.'

'You're very hospitable, thank you … So we can begin.'

She did not sit. Instead she spoke as she looked out at the vista before her – the rolling plains, the bushes, the mountains – at scenes far beyond all those. He listened intently, jotting key words in a notebook that would prod his memory when it came to writing his article.

She breathed of how the pomp and glamour of the military seduced naive and innocent girls – the gilding on the uniform, their martial bearing, their money. You'd think such sights were specially designed to lure away the hearts of young women. Their camping grounds and tents, the flags, the plumes in the helmets all excited a young heart, made it susceptible to love that wasn't love at all, or maybe it was a type of love but not of the variety that lasted. Pretty soon it turned out that the girl was not wanted by the soldier nor by her family and her little money ran out. Her clothes tattered and her belly crying for food, she turned to consorting. She got the disease and either worked with it until it maddened her or she put herself directly into the workhouse for a cure that sometimes took three months or longer to come about. And when cured, it took her much less time to win back what she'd shook off.

Silence, then.

'And that is what happens to them,' he said into the silence.

'Yes,' she said, breaking her gaze.

'Bridget, why are you here?'

'Much as I've already said. Circumstances – accident – love – men.'

'You followed a soldier.'

'I did. Indeed.'

'Is he…?'

'We'll fail to talk about the bastard, Mr Tone. Save to say a young man once loved me and he was a decent skin and I spurned him. I'm here because of that – because I loved a wicked man more. Do you see what I'm saying, Sir?'

'Yes.'

'Most of the wrens will tell you that it was a man who brought them here – indeed we have a poor young one with us four days now: Rosanna who's gone for the tae – she doesn't know which end of her is up.'

'A pretty girl? With stunning blue eyes?'

'A looker alright, with a bad cough and a weak constitution I dare say.'

'Here isn't good for her, so.'

'Where were we? Ah, I don't know … Regarding myself and why I'm here – 'tis my own fault, for believing one promise after another.'

'And the workhouse?'

'Oh Jay, no. To be slaving over a steaming laundry all day and listening to a priest talking to us about fallen women as though there were no such thing as fallen men. Not a drink to cross our lips … This is hell here, Mr Tone, but the workhouse is a different kind of hell.'

'I suppose you are right – but at least you would have a roof over your head.'

'A roof, aye, and a weight of piety.' He looked at his notebook and pocketed it and the pencil. He said, 'I best be going – I want to take in the scene where the nests were destroyed by the Ranger and his men.'

'Bad cess to them for doing the harm.'

Richard said quietly, 'Here, Bridget … to ease your cross.'

For a moment he thought the wild eyes of her were about to rip his hand off.

'A fine gentleman you are! A guinea. And, sure, I had little enough to tell you.'

'On the contrary; I learned more than a little.'

'A little learning can sometimes be too much.'

She stepped outside and he followed her. His kindness urged her into some more talking, 'Some of the girls married soldiers but they weren't allowed to live as husband and wife in the camp. Then the men were transferred to elsewhere or killed and, sure, they had no one then and did whatever they could to survive. Sure, we're simply trying to make enough money to keep ourselves alive. Do you understand, Mr Tone?'

'I do.'

That evening he did not delay at the dinner table as he was anxious to record his findings. He had a need to scratch his quill on paper, wanted to leave the furze and the woman on the page and not be carrying them around with him in his mind's eye.

He wrote of what she had told him and of some more that others had said.

The wrens give birth and die in their nests. They receive their families in them, if they visit. They wear a frieze skirt with nothing on top save another frieze around their shoulders. In the evenings the younger women go out to meet their soldiers in the uninhabited gorse patches wearing crinolines, petticoats and shoes and stockings. The older women remain behind to mind the children and to cook food. All the takings of a nest are pooled and the diet of potatoes, bread and milk are bought on the few days a week that the women are allowed into the camp market. They do not love the life of vice but prefer the squalor of it to that of the workhouse. It is a cold life that they lead ...

Though his thoughts and feelings had been committed to a region outside his being, there was no peace in his mind that night. He slept in a bed with a fire burning in the grate and a hot whiskey reaching the places the fire couldn't reach. Still the images were with him, and the smells too. Clinging to him like ghosts determined not to be exorcised.

CHAPTER 15

JAMES DISMOUNTED from the piebald and stood by its flank for seconds, looking at the scald crows and a trio of magpies at their feast, chased away by a mangy dog with ribs showing like accordion rills. Sheep bleated and scattered in protest as James walked through the flock on his way to the scorched furze, the dog dipping his snout into the exposed and raw flank of a dead sheep.

'Away with ye now, badgering the sheep; off ya go! Scat!'

He threw a stone, then another, catching the dog in the ribs. The brindle mongrel yelped and scudded away, tail lowered. James stood over the dead sheep and shook his head, not pitying the creature but considering the task of its disposal. He rubbed the back of his neck.

'One of Daly's,' he said to himself on seeing the red dye.

Hauling the sheep deep into the nearest furze bush, he left it there, knowing the flesh wouldn't be long left on its bones; not with the foxes and rats, the hungry dogs and scavenger birds.

He returned to the camp before noon, tethered the horse to an iron hoop protruding from a wall in the yard and went to see Kennedy in his office. Kennedy had the tip of his finger in his nostril. James could not reconcile the image with that of the clean man that Kennedy usually presented.

He removed his finger and said, 'Well, James, is the news true?'

'Aye – a bayonet set into it all right.'

Kennedy sighed and said, 'I don't know. I just don't know.'

James watched as Kennedy stood and arched his hands on his lower back and moved to the window, leaned his back to the narrow rim of sill. He turned his gaze then to the brown leather chair that rightfully was his.

'My back is beat,' Kennedy said to the floor, then again to the outside world that was fast losing the leaves from its trees. He stared at James, like he was measuring him for something.

'From the fall?' James said.

'Aye, since then; since I slipped on the icy path.'

'There's a man I know who can fix –'

'A quack. Been to him, James, been to him, no good – nothing does me any good.'

Silence then, apart from the ticking of rain against the window.

'No clue as to the soldier's regiment?' Kennedy asked.

'None.'

Feck would I tell you if I knew, James thought, sitting to the hard chair by the tepid stove. The soldier would get seven shades of bad punishment and for what? Making a point? A lump of mutton, it cost, to protest at the burning of the wrens' nests and give warning to the farmer not to go complaining to us or the Provost Marshal about the wrens and their business affairs.

Kennedy turned about, his face full of pain. James believed that most of this was feigned: that the pains came at him whenever it coincided with a desire of his to visit his brother's widow in Dingle.

'How many of them are on the plains, James? The Provost Marshal will be asking this of me when I attend a meeting with him presently.'

'My last count was 513 of a flock but that was in the summer. Come winter the figure is more than halved. Who'd winter on the plain only the sheep? The wind is too severe, the landscape no shelter against it.'

'Awful,' Kennedy said. 'What action will bring us to a complete riddance of them?' He inched across the floor, wincing as he moved. He smelled of liniment, something like menthol. He removed his coat and brim hat from a hook on the back of the door and said, 'James, I shan't be long. You rest yourself there a while, for God knows what you'll be at in the afternoon.'

He closed the door behind him gently. James waited a few seconds and then hurried to the window to ensure Kennedy had left the yard, that there was no fear of him returning to collect something he had forgotten. He sat on the leather chair, put his elbows on the table, rammed a finger into his nostril and out again and helped himself to one of Kennedy's powdered boiled sweets that he kept in a glass jar beside his quill-holder and ink bottle.

'Fecker, that lad,' he muttered, 'snot-picker like him I'll not be.'

Kennedy knew nothing of living life in the open. James had the experience of a week that first time he left his father's roof. His mother had been alive then, and she had begged him not to go. He thought, 'My balls were frozen to the size of peas ...'

He had arched his back to the fall of snow so it would build on him and keep him warm. If he had stayed outdoors longer than a week he'd have been frozen to death. Last winter he had come across four women in a hole in the ground that they'd scooped out for themselves. Begging him for a few bob, they saluted him when he gave it and said, 'God be good to you; it'll buy us a bottle of whiskey.'

Kennedy often called the women 'them'. He said it with a turn of lip that revealed some of the true measure of disgust he felt for these women. Others called the women by different names: unfortunates, fallen women, nightwalkers, prostitutes, wrens. James was sure that if Kennedy got his fat rump out from his desk and traversed the plains he would, in his travels, meet with a dead wren. He himself had done so on three occasions. Exhausted, tired and cold through – debased by themselves, by others and by destiny's fickle heart which James felt certain could only be owned by a priest or some other kind versed in sums and books but not in compassion.

'Perhaps,' he murmured to himself, 'it's time to patch things up with the oul fella and go home to run the family farm.'

There would be no burning people out of sorry dwelling places, no harrying of souls, no picking corpses off a thistle floor.

He leaned back in the chair, taking the front legs off the floor. The slatted ceiling with its tear of wood, the edge of a stack of old documents visible. The attic, a storage space for old files and records, was reached via a trap in the outer office, the public reception area. The timber was rotting. It occurred to James that the whole place was rotting away. He got to his feet and searched the drawers for information worth reading. He had let Kennedy away with thinking that he couldn't read at all, but he could, a little. There was nothing of interest. A stray notion lighted on him: Kennedy no longer left notes lying around. James tried to remember a time when he'd read something in the man's presence – he must have done. Kennedy missed no trick. Wide awake to the world.

Chapter 16

THE WALK was proving sore on her feet; she felt a blister rising on her heel – sore yokes, but once the bubble was full she could heat a sewing needle and burst it. Till her return to the nest she would just have to maintain a silent lip.

She espied two cavalrymen in the distance and her heart leaped. Johnny, out looking for me? She saw more mounted men away to her left and right and the quick notion she had of following and calling after the first pair she'd spotted was dashed. 'Hopeless,' she said to herself. Don't they all look the same from a distance, in their red and whites?

Newbridge, Bridget had told her, was a place for a wren to get in and out of in a hurry, for the people there weren't kind to fallen angels; no town was, hereabouts. Along the wide street she walked, all the shops on one side, the barracks on the other. There were nice things in the shop windows. Clothes and perfumes and a hat with a pink ribbon that she liked.

Tea leaves was all she had money for. She thought of crossing the far side of the street to inquire of Johnny in the barracks but told herself that he had said he'd be in the Curragh and that he wouldn't say it if it weren't true. A series of ponies and traps passed by on the road – a donkey and cart, too. The ground was littered with mounds of fresh dung and old dung that had dried and was breaking up into what looked like large tobacco flakes. She sighed and walked into a shop, her fingers tight on her money.

The tinkle of a doorbell brought up the eyes of the shopkeeper from his brass weighing scales. He fixed her a hard stare and averted his eyes to the customer he was serving, muttered something to him. He tied up the customer's package and gave him a farthing in change. The stout man on his way out gave Rosanna a wide berth. Rosanna brought in a deep breath of the shop's spicy and meaty air and inched forward to the long varnished counter, its surface black in places and worn in others, the grains running long in arrowhead patterns. She knew this without having to scrutinise, for counters are counters no matter where. The small cup bell over the door announced a departure and within a second an arrival. Then another. She let the woman behind her go ahead, out of courtesy, used to doing so for her betters. I'd love money on me to buy something new and nice, something, anything, she thought, for cheer.

She waited her turn to be served, aware of the young gentleman behind her. She thought of the night she had had – a night spent shivering with the cold and Peggy snoring and Bridget and Violet talking half the night. If Johnny did not arrive soon, she had resolved to search for him. She would not depend on Bridget to bring him to her, nor would she be put off by the Ranger.

Tentatively she approached the counter. The shopkeeper was dressed in a brown apron. He had thick forearms and almost no neck. His hair was heavily oiled and there was no charm in his eyes; there was a mist in them and she wondered if he looked at the world through cloud.

'Can I have a half-ounce of tea, please?' she said.

'Tea is it? Indeed.'

'Tea, yes, please.'

His hand went high and stormed hard to the counter. She recoiled at its smack, the venom in those green eyes.

'I will not serve tea to you or your kind. Now get out before I call for the constable.'

'A half-ounce is all …'

'Not if you were dying would I give it. Out!'

She backed away a couple of steps and then fled to the street, shaking at his treatment. She stood outside the shop wondering where she should go next when a young man followed her out and handed her a paper bag of tea. He refused to take her money and said, 'Isn't it a grey day for the country when a soul owning a counter serves as judge and juror?' and then he was on his way.

'That's what Peggy would call a rale gentleman,' she murmured to herself.

She walked on a little, not entirely looking forward to the journey to the nest. She heard the hard fall of feet on the path behind her.

'You!'

The word shot through her. Though it was nameless, it carried her name. She felt as though something icy and shadowy had stepped into her body.

The shopkeeper, she thought, he wants his tea back. I swear.

'You there!'

She stopped walking and turned about and saw that it was a priest with a red face of fury. She did not see him raise the riding crop till it was too late.

It landed across her shoulder and the next blow crossed her face – he rained the crop on her and forced her to the ground.

'Stop, stop!' she cried.

She saw her blood come out of her in spurts and cried louder, aware of people gathering round, glimpsing the fine lady she had seen at the station.

Many things at once crossed her mind – she crawled away but he followed her and brought the crop to bear. She thought of her baby in her, suffering this as she was suffering.

'Stop! Jesus!' she called.

But he flayed her all the harder.

'Stop him, someone.'

But no help came from onlookers who stood as rooted as trees.

He lay the crop beside her and came down to his knees beside her, panting like a colicky horse after a five-furlong sprint. He leaned over her and took a scissors to her hair. Weak and sore as she was, she managed a feeble resistance that he crushed with a backhanded slap across her cheek. 'Dirty women – bad creatures the lot of ye!' he roared as he slashed her hair. When he was done he picked her up by the upper arm – strong as though he had all the power of Christ in him.

At the time she felt that pressure worst of all, for the helping had been cruelly done. The depth and hardness of his fingers.

'You are never again to set foot in Newbridge. Never sully its air with your filthy presence. Do you hear me? Do you?'

She went to answer but the blood in her mouth prevented her.

'Answer, damn you,' he said, showing her the crop like a rider out to exhaust his horse of its last reserves of energy.

'Yes, Father …'

CHAPTER 17

A DISTANT sound of gunfire came to their ears as though pushed back in their direction by the embankments of the rifle buttresses. A loud sound of cannon fire rent the air, stirring the linnets at the rear of the bushes into a flight of winged terror. Rosanna's eyes opened wide.

Bridget said, 'Shush, lie still there, 'tis only the soldiers at their rifle practice.' Rosanna's wide-eyed look half-frightened her.

Violet whispered, bringing a tin mug of water, 'I'm after telling James how she came back to us a terrible wreck.'

Bridget accepted the mug and brought it to Rosanna's lips.

'Jesus, she's a bad sight,' Violet said, after having a good close look at the patient.

Bridget sighed. A right bad sight alright, with the hair cut in chunks from her and her scalp marked where the points of the scissors had been dug in.

'I've never seen anyone get a worse bating,' Bridget said, 'the fierce welts on her, red tongues of hatred. Not an onlooker stood up for her, not even to utter a word of restraint. It says a lot for them, none if it any good.'

'I better be going. The men are waiting.'

'How many, Violet?'

'Three.'

'God, you'll be a busy girl.'

'Won't I? 'Tis better to be doing what I'm doing than lying there in a wicked heap of agony. I told them they've five minutes each, is all.'

'Off you go and take a far bush for I don't want to be hearing ye at it.'

Violet said, 'Okay. Be seeing youse.'

'Be seeing you.'

Bridget popped a cork from a bottle.

'This'll hurt, Rosanna, but it's a good balm, it'll kill any infection.'

'I want to see Johnny. Will you send for him?'

'Shush now; don't be talking.'

'Bridget.'

'I think he's away with his regiment. I am sure he –'

'Please, Bridget.'

'Sure, 'tis no hurry – you don't want him to see you at your worst, do you?'

'I can't stay here Bridget, I can't. He loves me, Bridget, he has to come. He wouldn't want to be putting me through this. He must get leave – he can get that, isn't that so? If only for a few hours to show me where he has our place.'

'He said that ... he has a place for you?'

'Yes.'

Aisy with this one now, Bridget thought; she's a rare China cup in your hands and yours aren't the safest of hands to be carrying anything that's prized.

'Okay so, Rosanna, I'll get him.'

'He's probably looking everywhere for me.'

'No doubt. There won't be a priest safe when he finds out what's become of you – a head of steam, he'll have.'

Bridget fell into a deep silence. Should she tell her? Is this the time for it? No. But then there's no good time to be told bad news.

'Rosanna?'

'Hmm.'

'There is something you need to know.'

69

'Is it about Johnny? Is he okay? He's not hurt – he's not, is he?'

Bridget sighed long and hard.

'What?'

'Your baby – you've lost the wee handful.'

'No … no … no!'

'Shush now, shush – the babby wasn't intended for the world and it's best you forget about it and –'

'Please, no!'

'You poor thing … but I've seen others in your state and you have to live and get on with things. It's what we do. We –'

Rosanna said fiercely, 'Why is it best that I forget about Samuel?'

Bridget backed away. 'Johnny … you need him. He'll be here – we'll put the word strong that he's to come see you.'

CHAPTER 18

FOR A while his thoughts refused to form with any degree of clarity and arrangement and when finally he managed to bring them to order they did not transfer well to paper. Page after page he crumpled into a ball and fed into the wastepaper basket. Once, he had plucked something from the basket in a desperate hope that he had been too harsh in his estimation of the piece and it might prove to be of sufficient quality that he might peg the rest of the narrative upon it. His original assessment, spontaneous as it had been, was correct.

His latest endeavour wrought from him a loud sigh of exasperation. He drummed his fingers on the desk, a dance of indigo-stained fingertips on the walnut's grainy pattern. His shadow hung bent over the wall, strong and dark in the glimmer from an oil lamp; the fireplace dim under a weight of wet smouldering slack.

I shall try once more, he said, more to his shadow than himself, picking up his quill like a mason would do his hammer in sheer determination to wreck a stubborn rock.

He wrote and replenished the nib…sentences along, the words coming:

> The nests have an interior space of about nine feet by seven feet and there is no standing room till you crawl out again. They are rough and misshapen domes of furze. There is no chimney, not even a hole in the roof, and the smoke from the turf fire which burns on the floor of the nest has to pass out at the door. The door is little more

than a veritable slit, kept open by two narrow posts, which also serve to support the roof. Sods of earth and strips of corrugated iron (much used in the military camp) are used as additional protection – this bush house fashioned by means of rearing a wall by piling and trampling of furze bushes that the women and perhaps a friendly soldier or two might cut down. A simple construction, perhaps adequate enough shelter in balmy weather but come winter the mud and furze components shift, shrink and melt and cave in on the wretched occupants…

He paused to gather more thoughts, more memories of that day's visit to Bridget, but as he leaned forward to continue writing, a searing pain came to him with such intensity that he could scarcely draw his breath and in tandem with this grew a raging fear of intolerably worse to come. He could not straighten himself. Clutching his side, he pushed back his chair and stood insofar as this was possible. He staggered to his bed and lay there, the action curbing the agony by degrees till he could breathe easily and the pain moderated to a nagging reminder that such tricks merely served to keep the storm clouds in abeyance for a while.

CHAPTER 19

JOHNNY CAME to see her two days after the beating. She was feeling a little stronger in herself. Sore all over but the sorest spot of all was in her heart. She knew he would come – when she saw him she filled up and though she had clutched her mother's locket beforehand and breathed a hundred prayers not to, she started to cry. He stood there awkwardly. Perhaps thinking of the cut of me, she thought, and in shock over it. Blaming himself and no blame held to him. I must look a sight!

'Johnny.'

'Stop your crying.'

Rosanna looked at him in the diffused light of the bush and wondered who was this stranger stood before her. Not the Johnny she knew.

'Why didn't you meet me at the station like you promised?'

'It went by my mind.'

'You were too busy, is that it?'

'I was. Fierce busy.'

He stood there like a tree with no branches to make a noise. Hunched over in the furze, hand rubbing his lips, moving his eyes everywhere except to Rosanna's.

'I have some terrible news for you, Johnny.'

'I can see your news – the collared lad gave you a bad hiding, all right.'

'That's not my news.'

'What is it?'

'Why are you staying your distance from me?'

'Your news?'

'I lost our baby.'

'Our … baby?'

She thought, I hope he doesn't go off the wall and go after that priest and do something to him that we'll all regret. 'He was to be a surprise – I was going to call him Samuel, after …'

She let her words trail off, for Johnny didn't seem too put out and she was reading his features hard, in the hope that she was reading him wrong.

He said, 'All's well that ends well.'

'Johnny?'

He moved toward her and she believed for a second that she hadn't been reading him the right way at all.

'Hold out your hand. Come on, I don't have much time. There's a couple of sovereigns in the bag that'll get you out of here. Close up your palm, for if the others see the shine of them you'll be left without an arm.'

The black leather bag of coins weighed like a cold stone.

'John –'

But he was going from her, the breeze of his turn a cold slap.

'Listen!' she said.

He stopped at the mouth of the nest but did not look back.

'I … we buried him under a lone hawthorn bush in a clearing in the furze about ten minutes' walk from here.'

'I have to be off. We have a review in an hour's time. I've a horse to groom as well as myself.'

She followed him outside, grabbed his elbow and called, 'Johnny!'

He shook her hand free with unnecessary force, 'Go away, for the love of Jesus, and leave me be.'

'What did I do wrong? You said you loved me. What'll I do?'

He whisked about on his heel and there was spittle on the edge of his mouth; for a moment she thought it was in him to wash her face with his foam.

'Do what the other women do.'

She fell silent. On he went in the dreary rain in his best boots and second-best uniform without once looking back. Do what the other women do.

Hurt and anger swelled up in her. This wasn't happening – he's not himself. No way, no way. She put her hands to her forehead, then her mouth. Without warning, Peggy lit on her and snatched the bag of coins.

Triumphantly she said, 'That bow-legged rat owes me for favours rendered.'

Bridget said, 'Peggy, give it back. That's her Dublin money.'

Violet said, 'Let's go have a sup the lot of us. Men and rats, bad tails the pair of them.'

Rosanna said through gritted teeth, 'Give me back Johnny's money.'

'I'll give you a belt in the gob, that's what I'll give you.'

Peggy walked away counting the money and, sick and weak as Rosanna was, she grabbed a hold of Peggy's long, straggly black hair and tugged on it, gripping hard.

Cries and threats Rosanna didn't heed and she swung Peggy by the hair, keeping her distance to prevent her taking advantage of the slack.

Peggy shrieked, 'I'll swing for you! Bridget get her off me – get her! Ow! Ow!'

Rosanna thought, don't let go of the bad bitch; rip the hair off her – oh Jaysus her hair has come away!

Bridget said, 'Holy Mother of God! Rosanna, stop! She won't have a root left in her head!'

'Oh merciful Jesus, the pain!'

Rosanna smiled – her smile louder than a shout for the others went stock-still.

Bridget spoke up, 'Violet…give me that. You haven't a good hand.'

She took the scissors and cut the strand free of Rosanna's hold and Peggy made a go for Rosanna, teeth bared and murderous intent in her eyes.

Bridget and Violet put themselves in front of Peggy, but she was struggling through the barrier.

Bridget shouted, 'Rosanna, get away from here, we can't hauld her forever. Go the feck, go on.'

And she went the way she came with nothing only the clothes she stood in, her locket, and a bad bout of coughing, all of her temper spent.

CHAPTER 20

HE HELD his hand to his mouth and breathed. A smell of mint from the sweet that Josie had advised him to suck on. His digestive system was never the best, a weakness passed on to him from his mother. The smell of its badness revealed itself in his mouth odour. But he was fine now; his tummy had settled, and he was in good fettle. Clouds had parted.

He moved his eyes to the slim vase of orange flowers on the sill. Josie poured a little wine in her glass and then held the neck of the bottle over his. He shook his head and gave a small wave of his hand to stem her usual insistence. He was sitting by the bay window, legs crossed, looking at the slip of lawn that ran to a curtain wall of the old keep which had the branch of a tree growing through stones thick and stout and well surviving its thrust. The power of the root, the drive towards light. The leaning wall with its curvature like a spine gone off course – a three-hundred-year-old spine.

Josie sipped at her wine and then set to smoking the room with a leaf of burning white sage. A faith healer told her it cured homes of bad spirits. She believed her house was haunted by a little girl who had fallen from a horse on the street outside their home. She had seen the girl on the landing and despite having had the house blessed by Father Taylor she believed the girl's presence still lingered.

'Supper?' Josie said, extinguishing the sage by waving it violently.

'Something light, perhaps,' he said, getting to his feet.

He followed her into the kitchen, through the gloomy hallway with its portrait paintings of people who knew how to take themselves seriously. Her late husband's people. Josie put the sage in the enamel sink and said, 'Roast beef or cheese?'

'Beef, cut thinly, Josie – thank you.'

They sat at the long maple table in silence. An oil lamp burned on a wall bracket, a small fire in a large fireplace with ornate surround hissed of wet coals and damp log.

'Are you finished your work here, Richard?' she said.

'Not quite.'

He wondered if she was weary of his presence and decided that she was, a little. His hard words with the priest had probably isolated her from an element of the community that she was fond of being part of. She had good time for a man undeserving of such loyalty.

'It's such a strange topic to write on, Richard, is it not?'

'More sad than strange.'

'I saw her a little while ago …'

'Who?'

'Your waif with the blue eyes.'

'Where?'

'In town.'

Josie brought the knife to bear on a slab of cheese.

As she cut through she said, 'He beat her till she was a sorry sight of herself, Richard.'

He swallowed a morsel of beef and though aware that a sliver had lodged between his back teeth, something he would ordinarily hasten a toothpick to, he deferred the action, too interested in pursuing his cousin for information.

'Who beat her?'

'Father Taylor.'

This news was of no real surprise to him.

'Why, Josie?'

'For being what she is.'

'And what did you think of him for doing that?'

Josie stopped cutting. She looked at him and then laid her slice of cheese on a side plate.

'Did you try to stop him, Josie? Did anyone?'

Josie's voice dimmed like a dying candlewick. 'The speed and ferocity of the attack took everyone by surprise and it was done with before any of us had woken from the shock.'

He doubted that even in the full of her senses Josie, or the others, would have intervened and told the priest to desist, but he did not voice his belief. 'He used a riding crop,' Josie said.

Richard sighed and said, 'And no one did anything to stop him.'

'No. It was as I've said.'

'That man needs to be taught a lesson.'

'He's a priest.'

'I am quite sure that there's more sin for him to deal with in these fine houses than there is happening on the Curragh plain, Josie.'

'I beg your pardon?'

'Mrs Lafferty and Mr Mulligan – married but not each other, cavorting whenever their respective partners are away.'

'Who told you? Mr Lynch? He talks too much.'

'And Mr Brooks, the solicitor, who put the handle of a brush up a young chimney sweep's rectum.'

'How dare you say those things in front of me? Have you lost the run of your senses? Really, Richard!'

'And Olive O'Leary, the young woman raped by a neighbour of yours, a fact kept hidden from the law because money exchanged hands.'

'Mr Lynch,' she said, 'will end up talking himself out of a job.'

'Leave the car man be, for I heard more in the alehouse than I did from him.'

'Keep your talk for the alehouse – this isn't one.'

'Don't be blind to what's going on around you, Josie,' he said, pushing back his chair, plucking a toothpick from a small jar and adding, 'Good night.'

There was no reply.

Sleep would not come to him and his stomach was at play. The poor unfortunate on the grasslands in furze, let down by love and hammered by those from whom she should be receiving assistance. Josie – so judgemental of the prostitutes and so silent about the other activities. It seems that once sins are housed under a roof they are tolerable. He had that day visited the workhouse to see for himself the reasons why the wrens were reluctant to go there. And he could not agree with their argument that life without its walls was better – here they had proper shelter, access to medicines and food. He thought the restriction on their liberty was much too much for some of the wrens to bear as well as the feeling their carers gave off that they were minding the dirt and dregs of society. The wrens did not need someone to stoke the fire of their humiliation and degradation. He well understood why a woman like Bridget, for instance, would rebel against this insinuation – the women must be left with some scrap of their dignity intact if places like the workhouse were to succeed in their objectives. But with the blessed hand of the clergy involved he saw no easy solution for the women.

The shelters, he thought – lean-tos best fitted for animals and though assured that this was a temporary measure, he doubted it.

Rosanna. He thought to get up and write some more but his mind was too disturbed and so he remained in bed, not wanting to be there either. He found the night empty and full of a keening sort of loneliness.

He had not married. He thought of the woman he was to spend his days with, her long and lingering death by consumption, the rose-red quilt of blood in the last days. The ring he gave her had become too large for her. He'd watched her leaving him slowly, drifting from the shore of his heart.

The sound of a train in the distance, faint echo of people journeying elsewhere, like the loves of his life. Always a reason for them to be gone from him, always a reason not to stay – the lure of him not enough. This was it for him.

Alone.

His writings.

His social conscience.

His bad stomach.

His way of trying to change the world.

Small nothings.

Chapter 21

HE SAW her fix herself as she left the gorse and slowed in his walk to see if a man emerged after her. None.

He gathered that she had been at her toiletry and not the sad but profitable business. He thought her a good-looking woman. She had a good shape to her behind; the rest of her, scrawny but well rounded at the front for one so slight. He was aware that in normal circumstances he wouldn't have come close to having her as his lover. In their different ways they were both at odds with the world.

James hurried after her. A calm evening, not a breeze, the skies beginning to fill with stars and the moon full of itself. When he got close enough to her he called her name. She turned about, a worried look giving way to a slow burning smile of recognition.

He said, 'Will ye hold your horses and I'll walk with you a bit.'

He noticed that she had her fingers behind her collar at her throat as though checking herself for a lump, or was it where she kept her earnings?

An upbeat Rosanna said, 'Mr Ranger, good evening to you. 'Tis well you're looking.'

'Out for a stroll, are you?' he said.

'Is it not obvious?'

Cheeky smile on her. Full of mischief. Wasn't like that when I first encountered her on the plain. The lost look has gone off her. She knows where she is.

They walked alongside each other. He caught the scent of her perfume, something like honeysuckle.

'You've moved house, I believe,' he said.

'I have. Five weeks ago.'

'On account of Peggy I'd say.'

She said nothing and he did not press. An evening dew was beginning to fall. She broke out in a fit of coughing, a cough that worsened the aches in her.

'Have you no horse with you today?' she said.

'Your eyes are in better shape than your lungs.'

'And don't you forget it, Mr Ranger.'

'I like to walk by times.'

'You don't need to be looking down on things from a height all the time.'

Oh, the cheeky get. He found himself warming to her and asked himself if she was genuinely fond of him and then answered in the same thought: it's the game the others play, James, wake yourself man.

'That's true. I like to get down and dirty.'

'Do you now? So you're going visiting?'

'Visiting?'

'A nest, Mr Greaney. I hear you like to visit now and then. As well as to collect your little bit of rent.'

'Doing the business is what I call it.'

'Is it?'

'The rent is for favours rendered – giving youse advance warning of any evictions and telling my boss youse have gone from a place when youse have not. It's a risk I take, doing all that. I do sell things for some of youse as well and fetch a better price because my station is good.'

'Sure, I know it and we're entirely grateful to you. It's a good thing you do.'

So she understands that much – that I'm not the entire scoundrel that my hidden works make me out to be.

'It is, I suppose, a small good thing.'

A lull then, the song of a bird in a bush, not pleasant, too raucous.

'Is there anything that I can do for you, Mr Ranger?'

'God now, there is – there is – I–'

'So you've a want, do you?'

'A need.'

'A need, so. Grand. Have you money?'

'Certainly. I'm not a mean man.'

''Tis not much point in bringing a need home with you.'

'No, there is not.'

He heard the wheeze of her intake of breath. Like she was swallowing what she intended doing before setting herself to the act.

'Are you sound with this?' he said.

'Who usually does you?'

'I used to be with the Delahunty one, Ann.'

'She's good-looking. But she has the pox, you know that?'

'I didn't – but 'tis no great surprise.'

'Have you… ?'

'An itch … a sore.'

She nodded.

'You'll be looking, so there's no sense in lying, Rosanna.'

'True for you – but it'll do us no harm, the harm being already done.'

'You also?'

'It's a little something a rale gentleman gave me. Surprising the amount of rale gentlemen who come visiting.'

I see them and they never think that I do, he thought.

'There's a furze … It's free; a nice spot – we'll make for there,' she said.

'Grand.'

'Have you a wife?'

'No.'

'A sweetheart?'

'No.'

A sweetheart? he thought. Would I be here if I had? Most likely … most likely.

'That is something, I suppose.'

'It makes me a proper and not a rale gentleman, does it?'

'I wouldn't go so far as to say that. A nice man – you're a decent man.'

'I brought a bottle along.'

'Good – it'll help my cough.'

'There's something that you should know.'

'And what is it?'

'They're going to shift ye, the lot of ye in a few days or so – they're determined to rid ye off the plains.'

'They're always determined.'

'There'll be big fines and the like and ye'll have no choice but to face into the gaol or the workhouse.'

They arrived at the furze and she led the way through along the trail, the briars touching off each other, to a clearing that was mossy and soft and already wet with dew. 'Big fines,' he said.

'Ah, stop telling me bad news, will you? And don't you think you'll be charging me for it either …'

'I won't, on this occasion.'

'Why have they got the extra determination?'

'It came about because one of youse stole from a widow – her money, her jewellery, her clothes, a luggage case, the works – cleaned her out while she was away pouring her tears over her husband's grave.'

'It might not have been one of us.'

'No, that's true, but someone saw a dress of the widow's on

the train. The widow's curse will follow her. That'll be her punishment.'

Rosanna looked to the side and whispered, 'Such nonsense.'

'What is it you said?' James asked.

'I said to myself, is this man ever going to make a move for it?'

James nodded. He was hesitant, he knew. Uncertain. Though she was the same girl he'd run to Bridget she was not the same person at all, or was but her real self was somewhere deep within and no longer exposed to the world.

He watched her lay the length of herself on the grass and smile at him. She opened her legs ever so slightly. Unbuttoning her top, she exposed her breasts. Soft, round, ripe, nipples wine-coloured and like miniature corks. His fingers searched for his belt.

After they had finished she stood up and buttoned her clothes, held out her hand that he crossed with a little more than the usual worth of such pleasure.

'There's a sing-song at Athgarvan nests,' he said, asking in the way of not asking.

'I won't be going there. There's Peggy and besides, they lose the run of themselves at those events. Or so I heard tell. I keep to myself insofar as I can.'

'Peggy's away.'

'How do you know?'

'I was talking to her – some gentleman from Dublin she knows. I'll mind ye. Come on along.'

'Okay.'

She was flushed from the sex and giddy from the swigs of whiskey he had given her, loosening up no end, talking about her life in Dublin, her parents and little sister, how badly Johnny let her down. James thought that perhaps he should have let her go her way after the business because the drink in her had brought up her problems and he had enough of his own to be dealing with. For instance, Kennedy milking him and the way he had lately taken to keeping things secret from him, like movements against the nests – he was getting to hear of them from other sources. He was beginning to dislike Kennedy with some measure of intensity. His old man had not replied to his letter either, about working the farm with him on a level footing, to forget the rows of the past.

As they approached the Athgarvan nests they heard the noisiness and stopped walking.

'Shush,' he said, straining his ears.

Shouting and roaring going on there, he thought, perhaps we should shy away from it. It's not at all friendly-sounding – a bad air to the night, now.

'I think I'll give that place a miss,' he said.

'Me too.'

'But we might steal ourselves a look at what's going on; what do you say?'

'I'm game.'

She coughed and he looked at her. There's no shifting that, he thought and felt sad at this truth; he took her hand and squeezed it and saw by her reaction that there was both pleasure and fear in this for her.

'Let's go,' he said, 'real aisy.'

They went up the grassy flank of a gorse-shrouded hill that overlooked a natural amphitheatre where Donnelly had bludgeoned an English champion to defeat in one of many bare-fisted contests held there, where the soldiers these days occasionally met to sort out differences.

He made himself low and went into the furze, keeping her behind him, and crawled toward a vantage point from where they could see all that the moonlight and firelight would afford.

No singing of bawdry songs going on, but something that ran his blood cold.

'Something is not right, James,' Rosanna breathed.

He knew that she was not speaking of their spying actions.

He came to the edge of the furze and paused, then crept along the small margin of grass and peered down on the encampment. Rosanna eased alongside him. He felt her hip pressing against him, her fingers landing on the small of his back.

Naked men and women, drunk out of their skulls, dancing and baying at the full moon, an orgy under the magnesium glow. A fat woman astride a thin man licked at the blood oozing from his wrist, raised her head and looked to the heavens, howling and gyrating her hips on the still, thin figure, leaning forward over him to accommodate a man mounting her from behind. The baying ceased and all that happened now was the orgy – the grunting of men, the whining sounds of pleasure from the women, partners leaving one for another. He squinted.

'I want to go, James,' Rosanna said.

'Yes. We've enough madness in our lives without this.'

He accompanied her to her nest and stayed a while with her. Most of the neighbouring bushes were vacant. A child cried herself to sleep in one of them. Dogs howled and barked and he thought that, this night, the whole world had gone utterly crazy. 'I won't charge you this time,' Rosanna said quietly.

They lay together, naked in the comfort of the nest, such as it allowed, a poor fire hissing and sparking, and he understood that they both had a discomfort of the mind that a coupling would not banish.

'No, let's just lie like this, Rosanna – for the heat, only.'

In the soft sigh of her release he knew that he had done and said a most decent thing, for she would have given herself to him in order to save herself from being alone and so that she could forget about what they had witnessed, and perhaps dream of a better life in the cosiness of their commingled heat.

And it was also in him not to spend the night on his own. Rather there than in his quarters tossing and turning the night with his thoughts on the company of wolves and a fat woman astride a dead man. There would be ructions when the deed was discovered, he knew – Kennedy and the Provost Marshall would want to apprehend the culprits. He'd thought that he had the measure of the world and its ways but he knew then that he would never amount to anything more than an innocent abroad.

A long and tortuous sigh escaped him. He was certain that he had the measure of nothing in this life. Least of all himself.

Chapter 22

HE WATCHED the locomotive nose through the tunnel in a breath of steam and glanced at the timepiece that was a drop of silver outside the small pocket of his waistcoat. The squealing of brakes he found near-deafening and aggravating.

Thirty minutes late, he told himself.

Never late, Josie had said.

The train had more empty compartments than full.

Boarding the fourth carriage, he entered the first compartment and after settling himself he made to introduce himself to his fellow passengers.

'Bridget?'

''Tis yourself, Mr Tone.'

'Bridget … you're flying from the nest.'

'I am. I gathered my odds and ends and left. I couldn't face into another winter here – three on the trot, it would be. I've a few pounds in my purse and new clothes, the property of a widow with one eye – a decent and charitable woman. These will lend an air of respectability to me. I've an elderly cousin in Dublin who's lately a widower … and sure he might be glad of the company and what else.'

A woman with sense, he thought. 'I think you've made a very wise decision.'

A series of doors slammed shut followed by a loud and long whistle blast. The train lurched forward and stopped and lurched again before gradually building up a rhythm, chugging toward full flight.

Neither said anything for moments, each staring through the dusty windows at a river and a small island it surrounded. Then they looked at each other.

'Tell me, Mr Tone, do I look like a proper lady?'

'You're the finest-looking woman in this carriage.'

She laughed.

'What's so funny?'

'I'm the only woman in it.'

'You're a most respectable-looking woman.'

'You're too kind.'

'No, no I'm not. There are times when I can be most unkind.'

'We all have our lapses.'

'Did the others mind you leaving?'

Bridget pulled a face, 'I said nothing to them. Well, you couldn't tell Peggy because she'd leave you with a smile across your throat and Violet would have told her – poor Violet … she'll take the brunt of your woman's rages now.'

'That other young girl, the one the priest…'

'She's after spreading her wings to another nest. God love her.'

Before he had a chance to question her further about Rosanna she said, 'Are you back to London with yourself?'

He shook his head and said, 'No, I need to see a physician.'

'Are you poorly?'

He did not permit the wry smile in his thoughts to filter into an expression. 'My stomach is giving me much reason for consternation.'

'Ah, God love you – it'll be nothing. And if it is they'll fix it.'

Fix blood leaking from a place where it shouldn't? I doubt it very much. But one does not know anything for sure till one is told for definite.

She went digging in her bag and smiled when she found it, 'Here you go.'

'This is?' he said.

'Holy mother of Jesus, what does it look like to you?'

'A religious …'

'A small scapular.'

'I see.'

''Tis for wearing around your neck.'

'And this will help me?'

'Oh, Jesus, for sure. It's blessed.'

He smiled.

'Don't mock – didn't it get me out of a rich bind?'

He thought of mentioning that it was the widow who had done so, but Bridget would no doubt say this was providence. They chatted for the duration of the journey and when they reached their destination he bade her goodbye and said he hoped she had a better life for herself in Dublin. She said, 'If you see me in the Curragh again it'll be as a ghost; neither for love nor money would I bring myself there. No.'

Ironically, he thought, it was both which had brought and kept her there in the first instance.

Chapter 23

HIS TWO days in Dublin left him with three solid opinions, none of them favourable. There would be advice to be sought in London upon his return but he suspected he would hear nothing to afford him much solace. The latest in medication might bring a different date to bear on his headstone but would days spent in dreadful suffering count as days of living? he wondered.

He was not married and had no children and so his death would not impact on anyone to any great degree. What little money he had he intended to divide between his younger brother and sister, both of whom he loved and who were much closer to each other in age than they were to him. In truth, part of him had always felt more like a father to them than a brother. Their father had died when the ice cracked on the Thames. Though he was quickly brought to the surface, he died from secondary drowning: the lungs emptied of river water filled again. He had never forgotten death's determined call to their door and whenever his foot cracked a pane of ice his soul quaked.

There was a woman in London in the early days of a courtship that looked promising. This he determined to end abruptly without giving her the real reason – if told, she would volunteer to see him out and mean it, but the mere notion of being a burden dismayed him.

'Ticket, sir?' the conductor said, the brim of his peaked cap askew.

The question scattered his thoughts. A pity it didn't also put to flight his nagging pain.

Richard looked at the others in the compartment. Not a face

wanted to know his. The passing landscape showed the foothills of the Wicklow mountains, the snowy ridges, the farmlands, canals.

He must, of course, finish his article for Dickens and explain his premature retirement. He would do this in person for Mr Dickens; a lover of the written word prefers to hear them spoken to his face.

Mr Lynch met him at the Curragh siding – a grumpy, round-shouldered man who trusted no one and appeared by the hard set of his round face to dislike the entire human race.

'Good afternoon, Mr Lynch,' Richard said, stepping onto the trap and sitting alongside the coachman.

'Is it, sir?'

Richard smiled, 'Are you ever happy?'

'When I'm sipping ale, when I'm asleep, when I'm in the oul one – them are the times I'm happy. The rest of the time you can keep.'

'I see.'

'It's going to piss rain, sir – but I don't think we need the hood up just yet.'

'No, perhaps not … I want you to drop me on the Curragh.'

'Whereabouts exactly?'

'The nests.'

Lynch flicked the reins and said, 'Move, ye buggers – he wants the plains and I'm only an hour after washing the sheep shite off the wheels – no matter, eh, no fecking matter.'

He pulled up a quarter of a mile from the nests and said he was going no further because he didn't want to bring a disease home to the missus. Besides, the wrens would light on him like flies on dung to see what he wanted and if they could relieve him of his load for a sum.

'I'll wait and raise the hood – the skies are bad. You won't be long?'

'Go home, I'll follow.'

'I will not – Miss Josie would take a bite of my arse if I showed without you.'

'Tell her I wasn't on the train – that you'll go back to the station and check for my presence on the next one. Here.'

Richard pressed a coin into his palm.

'Right so … right – I'll go have a drink and call back in an hour.'

'That'll be better for us. I'd like to see you happy.'

Lynch scratched the corner of his mouth and said as though it hurt him to say, 'Them ones, sir … your tool will fall off you. I know a widow in town; now, she's pure fecking ugly and a big arse to her but … they're all the same in the dark, sir.'

'No, thank you.'

'Fine, so.'

He delayed a while when Lynch had gone before setting off to the nests. A slight breeze blew turf smoke to his nostrils and the first drops of rain had begun to fall. There was a loud cawing of birds and this noise gave way to the bleating of sheep. He began to walk.

'Hello! Anyone in there?' he said to the mouth of the nest he had been directed to by a half-naked old woman, empty of teeth.

He heard branches being disturbed. Movement from behind the hessian door. Like feet worn out by effort. 'I'm not game – will you come back Saturday? Please do.'

'That's not my business.'

A shuffling of feet, a loud bark of a cough, the soft swish of sackcloth being tugged aside.

'And what is your business?'

He looked at her and was immediately struck by her frailness, the paleness of her complexion. She'd gone down in herself in such a short time. Yet there was a glint of optimism in her eyes that her situation could get no worse for her and by this reasoning could only improve.

'I was told that you might be here. The third nest down, a woman said.'

'Do I know you?'

'Richard Tone. We met at the train station – the Curragh siding.'

'Yes … I remember … you were trying to make fun of me.'

'Ah … you'll forgive my behaviour, please?'

'That wasn't bad behaviour at all. The money gesture was nice. A saint's blessing on you for offering to part.'

'I was sorry you saw fit to decline the offer and the advice.'

She studied him with a keen interest that intrigued him. The look of a pedlar with a customer who might be interested in her wares, surmising a potential transaction. 'Step in … the wet has everywhere muddy.'

'It clings to boots.'

'Like a bad name to a woman.'

'I –'

She motioned him to a chair. The smell – God, how does she stick it? A cess pit, he thought. He sat on the legless chair. Rosanna remained standing, her arms folded across her chest, a thin blue shawl draped over her thin shoulders, clasped to her throat by a gossamer hand.

'You'll have tea?' she said, drawing his eyes to the blackened pot nesting in a weak fire of sticks.

'I'm fine, thank you –I'm not long after sipping.'

'So, what is it I can do for you?'

'I heard tell that you encountered a lunatic who was wielding a scissors.'

Rosanna lifted an eyebrow, 'Who told you? Was it your fine woman said it?

'My cousin, yes. She told me that it was a savage beating.'

'I glimpsed her, I did, looking at the scene.'

'She was horrified.'

'It's done with. I'm grand now – not a bother.'

'He is a complete brute.'

'It's a course of weeks since he beat me – already I'm over it. My hair is growing back and the wounds are healing.'

Not so well as she'd like me to believe, he thought.

'Rosanna … you're not angry at him?'

'Don't you think my hair is beautiful? It's really thick; run your fingers through it – you're more than welcome,' she teased.

Richard sighed.

'What?'

'Circumstances have forced you into living this life of vice – it doesn't necessarily follow that you are a bad woman.'

She breezed across the earth floor, kneeled at his feet and said, 'Smell this perfume off me – do I smell like a bad woman to you?'

He shook his head and breathed, 'No…'

'Well then – a pity for us I'm in the monthlies, isn't it?'

'I'm not given to …'

'To?'

'Consorting – I fear too greatly the disease.'

Fear? Why? For what reason? he asked himself. There is no longer a reason.

Rosanna said quietly, getting to her feet, 'I have no disease.'

He doubted if this were true. 'I have a little money with me today – I want you to have it. Buy a train ticket and leave here – go to Dublin.'

She went to speak but broke out in a fit of coughing. When she stopped she dried her eyes with the corner of her shawl and said, 'Whoa there, sir; I don't know anyone in Dublin. I don't know anyone there.'

'Take up the offer for God's sake, woman.'

'I will – the money end of things - but I'm not going anywhere, Mister Richard.'

This is a foolish woman, he thought, a thoroughly foolish young woman.

'Why not? It's not him – the soldier? He's a false dawn, Rosanna; surely you can see that by now?'

'Perhaps you're right.'

'Then?'

She stepped backwards till she met a wall of furze, 'There's always a hope that he might turn. I'm always having dreams that he comes to me and we go on walks with our baby.'

Her sudden dreaminess perturbed him.

'I buried him close by. Do you think he's an angel? One of the women said he wasn't because he hadn't been full born or baptised.'

Oh my God, he thought, realising it all so suddenly and so bleakly. She was clinging to a dead child, the residue of a dream that curdled into a nightmare.

'What does a man of great learning like yourself think on that?'

'Rosanna, I can tell you that he is most definitely an angel …'

'Yes. Yes … I have the strongest feeling that he is.'

'You don't need letters behind your name in order to listen to your heart, Rosanna.'

'True for you, Mr Tone. True for you. Now, will you come to see me on Saturday, you will? I'll give you a grand old time of it altogether.'

'I'm in bad shape, Rosanna, soon to turn worse. You are very pretty, but …' His words trailed off for he could think of nothing more to say on this matter.

'I think less about Johnny these days. There is a man I'm very fond of – he wanted to take me away but I wouldn't go with him.'

She said this in a dreamy sort of way and he doubted her veracity.

'So, Saturday,' she sighed, 'yes? No?'

'Is tea still on offer?'

'Most certainly – once you promise not to go on about me leaving.'

'Rosanna … Rosanna … Rosanna …'

'That's a lovely way to make a promise.'

It began to pour and the rain sieved through the roof and cast spits on the small fire that hissed and smoked in protest.

'You'll be staying till that's over,' Rosanna said.

Later that evening he wrote up his papers, thinking they were the last he would write of the wrens. His thoughts rambled and it was difficult to rein them into some semblance of order.

Rosanna, he wrote, told me she was afraid of Peggy, of the whipping the priest had given her. She showed me the marks on her back. The most remarkable thing was that she never said a bad word about the priest. Not one bad word did she utter. He cut her hair. That was worse than the hiding he gave her. She loved her hair. She loved her baby. The priest took him from her, too. I noticed that the light had gone from her eyes. She gave me the impression that she no longer cared if she lived or died. As Lynch said, 'She has the melancholy fierce bad.' Her body is riddled with cough and disease.

She talked of the skullers and what she and a man had seen at the hollow, the terrible things that unfolded. He lowered his quill; the ceramic inkwell was dry. His eyes were tired. Surely, he thought, she'd hallucinated. She would not divulge the name of the man who had accompanied her. He had asked her for it several times in order to check her story with him.

After replenishing the inkwell he dipped his quill and continued to write, not coherently but in the manner of note-taking, as though leaving thoughts on the page to assemble on another day.

A dead man – an act of orgy. And no newspaper mentioned it. What's abroad here? Vice and drunken revelry. Worse, if Rosanna is to be believed. Yet I spoke later with Kennedy, the

Head Ranger, and the Provost Marshal on the matter and they assured me that no such event had taken place. However, a question I put to them did cause them to look at each other with some small degree of consternation.

'How many deserters from camp each week?'

Many, it appeared – some of whom are never heard of again. But the point of this investigation will not be borne by myself. My time is already far too short. Mr Dickens will be keen to hear of this, no doubt; of necromancers baying at a full moon.

Chapter 24

KENNEDY SIGHED and commenced to chew on the nail of his small finger.

He had a habit of setting one fingernail to clean another and the clicking noise, though not severe, grated on James' nerves. Sprinklings of dandruff rested on the shoulders of his boss's waistcoat. Kennedy brushed at these in turn, his features rich with alarm and his mood dark and somewhat nervous – yet there was in him a sturdiness and a confidence that James had not seen before. Galvanised into action like a man with fire – like a man who is sure of something. Worry shaped itself in James, as slowly as the passing of beads through his mother's fingers as she recited the rosary – dead six years and not spared a tough ending despite her devoutness. What use is praying unless it's to find yourself the other side without your knowing how it happened?

Kennedy appeared not to have heard James' reply to the question he had poised moments earlier.

'So, you've been to the hollow and found nothing to report,' he said gruffly.

'I have.'

'And checked it thoroughly – up the flanks, into the very bones of the gorse?'

'Yes – insofar as it was possible. The briars are knitted and dense and it would take a good many men a fair while to hack through, to –'

'A pile of ashes and the ruins of a nest is all there is, you say?'

'Is all I found, like I've said.'

James watched Kennedy push his tongue to the side of his

cheek as though perhaps to nurse a bad tooth. He hadn't the manners to tell me what I was searching for, James thought – a grave; I knew it, but he wouldn't say. And why not?

'We had a report, James, from a press man about terrible ongoings at the hollow.'

'Ongoings?'

'Beastly things – unnatural.'

'Men with sheep? Like Trooper Daly?'

Kennedy's face filled with disgust, 'Aye. But murder and sexual intercourse with a corpse. Men and women crying up at the moon.'

James crossed himself. His face showed his disgust.

'Murder, Mr Kennedy?'

'Yes.'

'I was looking for a grave, so, and you wouldn't tell me,' James said, pushing his words through his teeth.

Kennedy frowned.

'Is there a reason why I wasn't told?'

Kennedy went to his desk, spread his tailcoats and sat down. He joined his fingers in a steeple and then pointed. 'You've been consorting with those filthy women, James – there are rumours circulating among the soldiers that you extort money from these creatures and sell articles for them. That, in essence, James, you are in league with them. I've mentioned this to you before, but the rumours persist.'

'All of it a lie – what else would you expect of them? A pig wouldn't speak kindly of its butcher, would it?'

Kennedy flapped his hands in placatory waves and spoke in a soothing voice, 'Which is exactly what I told the Provost Marshal that a good man's name was being blackened because he gave those women no comfort.'

He still has not mentioned the reason the search was kept from me, James thought.

'James, what do you know of the skullers?'

102

'Not much. I've heard the women speak of them – soldiers who don't want to pay for their pleasure, who rape the women. I've not actually met or spoken to a woman who has admitted to being so brutalised.'

'Not a gang, so – would you say that these are random attacks by a number of men who are not allies of each other?'

'Yes.'

'No grave?'

'No sign of disturbed earth, but they could have buried him elsewhere.'

'Him? I never said it was a man who had been killed.'

'I assumed, is all.'

'Assumed. The odds are strong for a murder victim being a woman, do you agree?'

'Yes.'

'I –'

'Do you suspect me of involvement?' James interrupted, on the back of small disbelieving laughter, his eyes remaining serious and coldly alert.

'No … good Lord, no.'

'Good.'

'Most likely it is prostitute talk and no more.'

James remained silent.

Kennedy nodded and said, 'James, we leave in ten minutes for the ridge of nests near the main road. This is the big push. I presume we won't find a string of empty hovels.'

'If we do, Mr Kennedy, I would suspect we have an informer in our midst and the clerks of the Provost Marshal's office need to be sorted.'

Their eyes met and held for a second.

'All right, James, you can go.'

James strode for the door and reached for the brass knob.

'Oh, James?'

'Yes,' he said, lazily facing his superior, affecting a nonplussed stance.

'A letter for you – it arrived yesterday evening.'

James crossed the floor and took the letter from Kennedy.

The oul fella, thank God, accepting my offer. May I be off this land of sheep shite and schemers in no time, he prayed.

In his sparsely furnished quarters across the yard, he opened the letter and held it to the window light. Not his father's handwriting, for it was too neat, too precise and in straight lines.

As a crooked line is no indicator of a person's uprightness neither does an upright one declare too much.

11th December 1863

My dear James,

Your proposition, though generous of you, is not one I think will serve us both in good stead. We are too alike and would be soon set at each other again. I also want to put you on notice that I have married Kitty Molloy and her sons will be coming to live with us and help out with managing the farm. A third young man's service is not required at present.

God be with you. Come visit when you have free time, when things have settled into routine here.

James Senior

Not his writing nor his words nor his intentions, James was sure. There was no doubt, the widow and her sons had influenced him. He regretted not having stayed put and weathering the storm he had with the oul fella.

He crumpled the letter into a ball and hurled it against the small pane. He saw the horses go by the window, the shiny wet boots of the troops and flanks of bay horses. He rubbed his lips and felt the frustration well within him. Things were losing their shape around here – moving beyond his control. He did not like this sensation at all, this sense of falling, of being frogmarched down a bad path. The sound of the rain was muted by the arrival of the horse column. He went outside and picked his sopping coat from the nail on which he'd hung it earlier. He stood under the porch and looked at the Provost Sergeant dismount and go in to speak with Kennedy. His piebald whinnied over the half-door of his stable.

'Aye, we're away again, boy, away again.'

He saddled his pony, mounted him and waited in the yard for the Provost Marshal to emerge, carrying whatever bad news Kennedy had told him of his Deputy Ranger. It was not lost on James that the Provost Marshal had not spared him a glance. He believed that Kennedy had spoken ill of him to this man. Kennedy was staying put to pick the dirt from under his fingernails, leaving it to others to do the real dirty work.

The rain was incessant, pushed at a sharp slant by an easterly wind.

They rode for a mile, increasing the gallop as they got within sight of the bush village. Some of the women who had spotted them on the horizon ran and shouted, alerting the others. They grabbed what they could and made off, but most emerged from their nests and stood to one side. The women hadn't heeded his warning because they had nowhere to go and could do nothing except hope that the rain might keep their antagonists at bay.

'Take them out – burn everything!' the Provost Sergeant shouted.

Dogs barked at the horses, a brindle dog loudest.

A few of the troop dismounted, lent their reins to their colleagues and spread flagons of paraffin inside the nests over whatever sad furniture they found. The fires took hold and started to eat the furze. The older women hanging about went to Cosgrove, the relief officer, who was parked nearby with two carts to convey the women to the workhouse. When the wagons began to turn their wheels most of the others followed in ones and twos, a ragged line of diseased and broken-spirited women, crying children.

Raindrops dripped from James' hat brim. He raised his collar and went to the rear and away from the company, eyes on the misery unfolding before him, tears forming – he was unsure whether they were for his own plight or that of the women. He feared too that some should approach him as they had done previously and blame or cajole him, saying things that would further cement the already well-grounded suspicions of him in others.

That bad feeling was still over him, like circumstances were running away with his life, like he had control over nothing any more and perhaps never had to begin with. He was a fool.

He spotted her then, wearing her blue shawl, looking up blank-faced at the warhorses, slowly walking to a bay horse that must have been at least seventeen hands. She said a few words to the cavalryman – silent words to James yet he read her lips and understood them perfectly. The horseman ignored her.

'Look at me!' she screamed.

He did not look.

'How can you do this? Shut me out like I was nothing to you!'

The man looked at her then and away. 'Look at me!'

James noted the churned earth, the desolation in her face, the unsheathing of a sword by the man, the raised blade and its fall on the nearest dog, severing half its neck. He saw that it could easily have been Rosanna's neck. The Provost Sergeant shrilled on his whistle and the men remounted and left. He followed them, driving his heels into his piebald, and when they turned for camp he kept going straight, for he had thoughts to dwell upon.

He had an image of muddied earth, of a slight thing stepping back from the man with the bloodied sword. Her mouth dropped open in shock. The dog wasn't mean or vicious. Charlie, its name was. Too tame to put a tooth in any living thing and barked only because it was expected of its kind.

He rode to a tavern not far from the hollow.

Chapter 25

WHEN THE plain had emptied of people she circled the ground where the hovels had been, a blackened margin of furze as the rain was too strong, the furze too wet for the oil to burn it all up. She touched her locket, clasping her hand around it as though there was a power in her dead mother's face that she could draw upon. A heat of love. She had been cleverer than the others by keeping a home amongst them, yet having another not too far away, within a couple of yards of a lone hawthorn, within sight of the tiny grave.

A traveller man of whom she had grown very fond in the weeks he had stayed hereabouts had taught her a survival skill in lieu of payment: he sourced semicircular iron bars and drove the spiked ends in the ground and draped a stretch of hessian over as a roof, taut and held in situ by skins of grass he had peeled away from the plains. Inside he put a deep bedding of hay he had stolen from the barn of a racing stable near the military cemetery on the hill. In the lair she was safe and warm and dry – enough space for her to sleep in comfort and for a small bag of possessions.

He was the only man who did something practical for her and wasn't full of himself, trying to cram notions into her head about leaving the plains. She loved his black beard and how he tickled her belly with it. He fashioned kettles and pans and trinkets and his dead eye and good eye were on her locket but he swore not to steal it though he assured her that he would have done had it been round a neck only a little less fine than hers. His name was Black Mellown and he played the fiddle and spilled stories through spoiled teeth. He lost his eye in a prize-fight or so he said, but he seemed too frail a creature to be involved in such a sport. Three weeks he stayed and she was sorry when he was gone – he left nothing and took nothing with him. He never buried his roots, he told her the night before he left, which was probably his way of saying goodbye. Perhaps 'twas just as well, she thought.

This is home. She did not do her business with the men in her lair, for the tinker man had told her that a body needed to have a place of its own away from all else.

Her nest was where she worked. To lie with the drink in her veins, a brute of a man inside her, her thoughts making him out to be her lover or blocking him entirely out of her mind, she brings herself elsewhere – walking in a park full of beautiful flowers with her baby in his pram; he moves his fingers and smiles at the angels that only babies and the truly innocent see and recognise.

Lately the cough is so bad it saps her energy even walking to her lair, she thinks. The itching in her was maddening. It never left her be. A fear of dying alone had grown in her and she suffered with nightmares about scald crows picking her eyes from her head as they did to dead sheep. She worried about the skullers. She lived apart from the other few wrens that remained on the plains. Bridget had left. Violet feared Peggy too much to dare walk off and leave her. Rosanna reached for the bottle and said, 'My only God-send in my peace place … Jesus, will you help me?'

She shouted, 'Will you do something decent by me for once! For once!'

Chapter 26

HE SPOTTED the priest from a long way off. There was no mistaking the torso that leaned forward as though struggling against a head wind, the hands behind the back, and the black garb.

Do I address him with stiff words? Or ignore? This wouldn't be fair to Josie who had merely set out to accompany him for a short stroll down by the river. A calm if cold day. Swans nested by the embankment and the river surged through a weir, coming at his ears like an angry shout in what had been an easy conversation. For two days he had lain in his bed, stomach in turmoil, and this morning the pain lay hidden behind a cloud of medication. He wanted to walk, to push his legs, to feel the air on his face, in his lungs. To feel alive.

'Richard – Father Taylor,' Josie whispered in warning.

'Yes, I saw his spectre moments ago.'

'And you saw fit not to tell me.'

'That is correct, Josie – and you know why I remained silent.'

He had said nothing for she would have insisted on their returning to Lynch who was parked outside the rusted gates. She would not risk being caught in the middle of warring tongues. Oh, for a Bridget beside me in this circumstance.

'Please, Richard,' she said, tightening her grip on his forearm.

He nodded. 'Please, Richard,' she said, tightening her grip on his forearm, 'say nothing.'

He nodded.

'I have to live here. You don't.'

Still, he could not resist saying something to *her*.

'You are quite safe, Josie; he has no riding crop.'

110

'His tongue is crop enough.'

By now the priest had spotted them. The path had reduced to a mere trail and neither party could pass by the other unless one stepped onto a verge of dock leaves and rushes.

'Good morning, Father,' Josie said without tremor in her tone.

How good women are at hiding things, Richard thought.

'And it is, a great morning – mild for the time of year.'

'Mild,' Richard said.

'And Mr Tone – how is our press man keeping these days? You must be writing a lengthy piece indeed.'

Josie said quickly, 'Richard has been poorly.'

The priest nodded slowly, 'I know by the pallor. Not good.'

'That's why we walk, Father, to draw in the air and get in some colour,' Richard said.

'Indeed, well, the river air will do that for you.'

He raised his forefinger as though to point to a thought that had at that instant occurred to him, 'Josie, can you attend the meeting next Tuesday evening? It's to organise a charity occasion to raise funds for the poor – you are the very best I have at my disposal for making a success of such a venture.'

'Certainly, Father.'

'Thank you, Josie.'

He tipped his hand to his forehead and stood sideways; in this fashion they passed by, exchanging goodbyes.

About twenty-five yards on, Josie breathed a slow release of anxiety. Glancing sidelong, he saw her shoulders climb down.

'Josie, you fret too much.'

'I was terrified at what you might say to him.'

'I was terrified at what you might *not* say.'

'He's a priest and entitled to our respect.'

'He's a man first and a priest second and no true man of God would –'

'Stop it, Richard. I won't hear you – if that girl wasn't what she was, then her back would not have tasted his ire.'

'Josie.'

She separated her hand from his forearm. 'While we're at odds I may as well tell you, Richard, that Doctor Flaherty has told me of the true worth of your health.'

'Has he indeed? Isn't that a dire breach of confidence?'

'Richard, I'm family.'

'You are, you are,' he said, taking her hand and addressing it to his forearm, 'and much treasured.'

'So, we must see to it that you receive the best of medical attention.'

'And some armies of prayers.'

'Richard …'

He suggested that they turn for Lynch. The pain was beginning to show from behind the cloud.

In the afternoon he was sound enough to read over his writings with a view to editing his verbosity. He began with a passage he was uncertain of submitting to Dickens's scrutiny.

I often see her in my mind's eye, on the plain and walking from the station in the downpour with her dreams in tatters – and I drove on by to a warm house and hot food because it was easier to do nothing than to do even a little … there are moments when I cannot sit still with myself.

A sweep of rain assailed the window and he looked in its direction. When his mind returned to the matter at hand, he did not omit or alter a single word.

CHAPTER 27

SHE WALKED like a woman who was full of the sores of the world. City fog was worse than the country sort, she thought: one thoroughly damp, the other damp and smoky. Either was good for chilling you to the marrow and giving you a barking cough that'd string you out to your grave.

Her lower back pained and the cold worsened the ache in her jaw. She moved in shoes that were two sizes too small towards a smoke-filled shop hidden down an alley the sun never lengthened on. The shop front held her attention for minutes with its display of a piano and stuffed foxes, squirrels and hawks encased in glass, a suit of armour and a rack of colourful dresses. Items for sale: their owners, no-shows.

It had been a while since her last visit. Barefooted or thin-soled, the cobblestones used to be acquainted with her step; the street's night lights acquainted too with her shadowy presence. A young strip of a thing taking men into her to feed herself, the drink numbing her against all their lies, their wanton usage of her body and in time hers of theirs. All sorts of men. A good one she let go for he wasn't what she wanted – he stone mad in love with her and she did nothing only mess him about and break his heart. She wondered what became of him, of her men, the ones she had had feelings for.

It got so she'd listen to their lies, believing them because she wanted so desperately to remove herself from her situation – taking a chance on a lie not being a lie, knowing it would not prove to be anything other – a true act of desperation.

The pawnbroker did not stir on his price for the goods she had spread on his counter, a wedge with patches of varnish worn off its veneer from the passing traffic of a million items of the down and out, the rich fallen on hard times and those in temporary crisis.

'Your father was a decent man,' she said.

'He was – but these things are … Look, have a gander in the cabinet behind you. I have brooches of all sorts and bangles and necklaces to beat the band.'

'These are top quality,' she said, forefinger nudging a pendant toward him.

'It's time for me to close up.'

'Okay … give me me due. And a pair of oul shoes – the bigger the better. I do have corns on me corns.'

'Shoes?'

'You've none.'

'I don't take in shoes.'

'There was a –'

'That time is long gone.'

'More's the pity.'

He swept the items into a straw basket and counted out her money in coinage.

'I take it you won't be back to reclaim these pieces.'

As shrewd as his oul lad. Shrewder even. Is there still the pile of deerskins out the back? His oul lad used to ride me on them and then go home to his missus and children – a daughter as young as myself back then – and peddle the lie of him being an upright citizen to all and sundry.

'I'm a seller,' she said, 'mostly.'

'Aye.'

She stood outside the shop under the yellowy gas light, nowhere to go. There was the tavern but she owed money for lodgings and the men had enough young ones to go around; they didn't need to spend their lust on a craggy-faced creature like her with a sagging bosom. If she went to her lodgings she would be in a worse plight than she was yesterday, her money paid over.

Two jobs she'd had in taverns in town but she couldn't keep a hand to herself, all that money coming across her and sure who'd miss a few of the coins? She had become used to lifting things that did not belong to her, a habit formed and done without thought. Missed their bit of money all right, the fecks did, and Jeremy, her last boss, left her on her arse with a mighty blow to her jaw – swollen, it was, for a week and more. Her few teeth still ached from the knuckled impact.

The city had never wanted her. She thought that by coming here she would find a means back from a bad place. It wasn't so. She could end up as a gutter woman, picked up and hauled away to the surgeons. The last of her would be gone, sliced to oblivion. A right huzzah. She would not have her own grave – she would lie wherever they threw the bits of bodies they had no use for. Ride you inside out when the breath is in you, she thought, and cut you up to nothing when it's gone.

She had heard of what they did to Sally in that college place. Some said she was still alive when they went cutting and up she had sat and roared and promptly died from the shock.

Men, she thought; some of them didn't need knives to cut you open.

She heard the call of the station and wondered if there was a train soon to depart.

It was dark and windy when she arrived at the Curragh siding. She walked across the damp grass in the general direction of her old home, not sure if it was extant or what sort of reception she might receive.

A month of it, gone. Thirty days, it took, to land herself back to nothing.

A few pissdrops of rain began to fall as she neared the furze. She saw the lantern, its weak light like a devil's bad eye. She called out, 'Violet, Peggy … hello?'

'Let it be Violet,' she whispered.

It was.

'Ah the craytur,' she said as Violet came to her and hugged her and said, 'Oh, Bridget, where did you get to and why did you go and what has you back?'

'There are worse places than here,' she said.

Violet sat her to a form which was the sole change in the home she had left. She kicked off her shoes and sighed relief.

'The feet are cut off me,' she said, rubbing her arch.

'You're not working?' Bridget said, looking at a pot of porridge on a tease of a fire.

'No – I've given meself a day off.'

'Good for you.'

Violet spooned porridge into a wooden bowl and handed it to Bridget.

'You're an angel, you are,' Bridget said.

'Dublin wasn't for you then?' Violet asked, sitting beside her on the bench.

'No, it wasn't for me.'

'Where'll you go next?'

'I haven't a notion. But I don't want to spend winter here if I can help it. I do hate the snow, the way it boxes us in and the cold turning your snot hard.'

'There's not many of us left on the plains.'

'You've a grand nest here.'

'It's okay.'

'Would she mind if I stayed awhile, do you think?'

'She might. She was fierce put out that time you did a runner.'

'Aye …'

'If you had something to give her, it might settle her cough.'

'Oh, I can make a decent contribution towards my keep all right.'

'It was you who robbed the half-blind widow blind?'

'Who says so?'

'The crows, the sheep, the soldiers, them all. Peggy says if sheep shite could talk it'd say it was you.'

Bridget ate some porridge and chewed contemplatively.

'It was me,' she said flatly.

'You made things awfully hard for the lot of us.'

Oh Jaysus, I never thought of that happening, she thought.

'They came down on a lot of the nests fierce hard – we were lucky they let us be.'

'That's why I need a place to stay – they sent a sheriff after me, to my cousin's house, and he said I wasn't in and ran me out as soon as the street was clear.'

'Who told on you?'

'I don't know. I suppose it was obvious if I was about the Curragh before the widow was robbed and gone from it afterwards – people are good at figuring things out like that.'

'You've the sense to be wearing none of her clothes.'

'All gone, the same with the other stuff, lying in a pawn shop it is.'

'She might let you stay – if you can sweeten her.'

'And how is your woman's moods?'

'Bad, as usual – you heard about Rosanna?'

'No ... what happened to poor Rosanna?'

'Wait till I put some sticks on the fire.'

'The poor thing; gone, no doubt. Sure, we're all going to be gone someday. Maybe someone will explain the nonsense of life to us then,' Bridget said.

The sticks were already sparking by the time Violet rejoined her.

Chapter 28

HE IS in no humour for shaping his thoughts on paper. But he must. In spite of his illness there remains that compulsion to record matters. It is perhaps an instinct to strive for routine in spite of his dire straits. An attempt at denial.

He raises the light in the mantle lamp, sets a match to a candle on his desk and sifts through his notes – there was the night he had Lynch bring him to the nests … a night he had wanted to search out Rosanna but she was nowhere to be found.

Knowing well that the wrens were night-birds I wanted to see their true colours by candle-glimmer in their nest. I stayed till late with them. There were two in the nest to begin with and three more who, when they arrived, took off their gowns and petticoats and made seats of them. Then came the important question from the elder wren, Mary, 'What luck had ye?'

They totted up a poor amount. It was enough to make a man's heart bleed to hear the details and to see the actual money. So as to continue my observations a little later in a way agreeable to the women, I offered to stand them supper. The proposition was joyfully received and though late as it was, one of the wrens went away and presently returned with a loaf, some bacon, some tea, some sugar, a little milk and a can of water. I received in change the precise sum: two shillings and eight pence halfpenny …

He sighs, rests his quill and thinks, I am not able for this, not tonight … He knows it is a fatigue that the sleep of the living does not banish.

Chapter 29

JAMES WAS in his quarters after putting an armful of wet turf to dry beside the stove when the knocks came hard and fast to his door.

'Who is it?'

'Mrs Dolan.'

A seamstress who did much work for the military and kept his own clothes together too. He opened the door, thinking she was to report a dying sheep or a horse that had bolted from a yard.

'I came across a woman lying on the plains … I was out riding my pony. I think she's dead – you better hurry.'

He suspected that it was Rosanna.

'I'll see to it, Mrs Dolan; you work away home.'

It was turning out to be a bad day all round for James. The light was beginning to fade and the rain was almost solid of itself. Earlier Kennedy had been cool towards him because of his alleged association with the wrens. He was acting as judge and jury on the strength of suspicion alone. James considered that general opinion had sullied his reputation beyond redemption.

He rode quickly, digging his heels into the flanks of his piebald which reared its head a little to the side, taken by surprise at such uncustomary treatment. She was lying in the open.

'Whoa, steady boy, steady.'

He dismounted and carried her into the shelter of a furze and covered her with a sack he carried for whatever the women might have for him to flog. 'Rosanna,' he said, rocking her shoulder.

She opened her eyes and moved her lips but her words were silent. Every inch of her was in a shiver.

'I'm going to get the pony and cart and I'll be back for you.'

'No.'

'You hould on tight, now – I won't be long.'

'No, no …'

He pushed the piebald hard across the plains, the rain causing him to squint, down the hill leading into Kildare town and up it till he came to Cosgrove's pub. Old man Cosgrove with the burgeoning stomach assured James he would proceed directly and bring her to the workhouse. James looked at him. He had said directly but made no sign of leaving his bar stool nor the full tankard of ale on the counter, his gaze fixed on it like it were a small treasure, the honey of his life.

'I'll take the pony and cart,' James said.

'You will not.'

'Then out the door before me.'

'Go then, if you've a mind. There's fresh hay in … she'll be soft and warm.'

Outside he tethered the piebald to the rear of the cart, climbed aboard the seat and tisked for the pony to stir itself.

The rain had lessened but the wind had turned crueller and he decided that he hated the landscape with its paltry shelter and rolling plains, its dips and hollows, its secrets, its military swagger, hated the noise of bugle call and cannon fire, the pennants and flags, the soldiers – the whole shebang he hated. He thought of America; he had enough for a passage and maybe the oul fella might stump him something for the pleasure of seeing him off his hands forever and thus banishing likely show-downs … he might.

Why wouldn't he?

He aimed for the hawthorn tree. Tree of the Druids – where the souls gather.

He brought the trap to a halt right beside the edge of the furze where Rosanna lay. Hurrying to her, he dropped to one knee and fixed his arms under her, 'Aisy, now – I'm here to bring you to the workhouse. You'll be grand – they have the stuff that'll see you right.'

He glimpsed the chain and locket and worked his fingers to it.

Rosanna lifted her hand but this was pulled back to her side by a harsh cough and a choking noise. 'No … no … stop – take your hands away – put me down.'

'Rosanna, for –'

'Leave me down … leave me be.'

'I can't.'

'Do.'

'Do you want to die?'

'No … but I won't leave my Samuel.'

Her who? he thought. Baby. Yes … She'd named him – sure the scut wasn't even born to be named. But – errah, there isn't time to think on that.

'I'll bring you someplace drier, then – is that okay with you?'

'To our place, Johnny?'

'Yes, where else, only our place?'

'Fine, so.'

He lifted her and walked to the cart. There was a small kick out of her that alarmed him.

'Rosanna…?'

A moment later.

'Rosanna?'

Chapter 30

KENNEDY WAS sick. To what extent James did not know. He had not reported into work yesterday nor today and word sent in by his wife was that he was poorly and unable to lift himself out of the bed. With luck, he thought, the bollocks might be lifted from the bed into his coffin.

A smoking steak and three tankards of frothy ale in the ale-house at the crossroads south of the camp had not mellowed his anger. The news contained in his father's letter had sparked a fire inside him that would not diminish and though there were times that his work occupied his mind, as soon as his time was his own again the fire raged. He harboured murderous notions and the only release he had was to imagine himself stealing into the farmhouse and slitting all their throats as they were sleeping.

It was an idea he would not put into practice for he was not the sort to exact that manner of revenge. His impotency in the face of such perceived injustice had formed a ball of hemp in his stomach. He was in a bind and had a bad idea that there was worse in store for him.

He saw her, then; there were women whose company he wouldn't have minded and a mere few he wouldn't want within a thousand yards of him – this slag was one of those few.

She eased onto the stool and said, 'I thought you were leaving – running back to your father and the farm?'

She had on a red dress and her black hair was shining, cheeks flushed. Eyes danced in her head, a mischievous twinkle in one.

'He was in communications with me, a letter saying that I was to stay where I was. It seems he's gotten himself a wife and two new sons.'

'Oh, that is bad news for yourself.'

'Don't I know it.'

'Did you let go of your work on the Curragh?'

'No, by the grace of God, I didn't open my mouth to tell them where they could put it.'

She smiled. 'Well then, all's not bad news for you.'

He stared at the tankard and brought it to his mouth. 'I could cheer you up,' she said, with a half-wink.

He licked his upper lip with his tongue and drew the back of his hand across his mouth and chin.

'No – I'm setting myself towards getting the painful treatment.'

'Is that so?'

She stood and went to him, tried to sit on his lap but he eased a distance between them.

'You aren't going for the treatment, James, you'd have to spend weeks in hospital – no pay for you and –'

'I'll buy you a drink.'

'Not ale. I'd soon drain a shot of whiskey.'

He called for Beckett to serve him.

'So, I see you're still on the plain,' he said to her.

'I am – hidden out of the way, bothering no one.'

'That may be, but they're still going to hunt youse out of there. Any day soon.'

'Bastards.'

'We are to you, I suppose. Surely you can see it coming?'

'Maybe I don't want to.'

'You should move your valuables to another furze … that way, you won't lose everything. Tell Violet the same.'

'You're a good man, James. Even though 'tis advice I was already on to.'

'A good man? I've heard that said before – a pity my old man doesn't think it of me.'

'Rosanna said it of you.'

'She did, aye.'

He resented Peggy mentioning her name. It didn't sound right. There was too much of a mocking ring.

'She was one stupid cow. Not for saying that of you, God forgive me, but for the way she carried on.'

He shrugged, looked at the scraps of steak on his plate. She spoke with her mouth half-full. 'Don't tell me you had a liking for her?' She put a finger to her teeth in chase of a sliver. 'You had – well now, so you had a liking for her. Maybe even more than that. Sure, God love you.'

Peggy laughed. She put her hand to the back of her head and shook out her hair. She probably thinks it tantalising, he thought, but 'tis far from an appealing action.

'It's not funny,' James said.

'She loved a fella called Johnny. I've had bad yokes lie with me but he was the worst. I don't how the hell she got mixed up with him. Mention his name to her and she went moon-eyed.'

'She was an innocent abroad.'

'For a little while.'

'Aye.'

'Aye,' she teased.

He wished hard for her to go. And she read his face in the way of women who have become practiced at reading men's faces.

'You'll have to excuse me now – a man who pays is after coming in.'

'Good night to you.'

She got to her feet and brushed her hands down her skirt. He did not envisage it staying below her knees for too much longer.

'I hear the priest who took a stick to her did the same again to

125

another poor yoke. If ever he comes near me I'll stick him, I will,' she said.

'Ah, God is sure to blow him a bad wind someday.'

'James – do you not know that God isn't on our side?'

He watched her sally to a table at the far end of the alehouse in an alcove more dimly lit than the others.

Moments later her raucous laughter reached his ears. A deal sealed in her rich appreciation of a man's joke or his ribald reply to what she could do for him. He contemplated the man; how, with Peggy, he might be facing into syphilis and the mercury injections and mumbled, 'Pray God it's only the pox that I have.'

He beckoned for another tankard and when it arrived he consumed it in great draughts and departed the alehouse a lot less sure-footed than when he had entered. He had valuable items in his bunk and wanted to sort and sack them in readiness for the ride to the pawnie in Naas come morning. That was the beauty of his job – no one questioned where he was because he rode the plains and no one could say differ. And if seen in Naas he could say he was visiting the workhouse to see what space was available for some more wrens. A good job, when Kennedy wasn't about. A good job, alright.

Chapter 31

VIOLET BROKE out a bottle while Bridget brought some hot ash outside and built up the dead fire that sat in a circle of stones. She pointed the nose of a bellows to the embers and squeezed, the air coming in a whiny sort of wheeze. She added more kindling and set thin strips of turf upright like old men leaning into each other to hear a dirty tale. Guests brazened to the heat: rats that each woman kicked at and shooed and thrashed at with sticks. A scabby mongrel, head lowered, inched closer, lay down and looked at the orange flames, taking the heat to his face. The rats and mice went out of sight but not out of earshot. Scratching of nails in a coffin, Bridget said. Violet shuddered and said for her not to speak of things like that.

Bridget swigged from the bottle and felt the liquor toast her lungs and belly. Takes the sting out of a lot of pain, she thought. She was agitated in herself, a great disturbance going on inside of her: anxiety, frustration, disappointment, sadness, anger – anger the stirrer. Her feet ached. She wore brogues given her by Violet, loose on her but the harm had been already done. The pain was shooting up her calf, travelling the prominent veins to her knees. She looked inwards at her rising temper, though Violet would later remark that she was looking straight ahead into the darkness. Briskly she whisked the ladle as though the content of the pot was a stew of her thoughts and not stringy lumps of cow meat.

'She'll be grand; don't be worrying about Peggy,' Violet said into the silence.

'I'm wondering if I should be off with myself and make a show in the morning?'

'No. I'm glad of the company.'

Neither spoke for a few minutes. Bridget studied the stars, the slip of moon, and felt a cold breeze wash across her face and brush her hair. She felt a strong need to piss but she was holding onto it for the heat because she was able; there were more rats than she'd seen before and the lidded chamberpot, a new acquisition, was full, so Violet said, with no sign of her setting to emptying it.

Violet said, 'I'd like to do what you did, Bridget, and get away from here.'

It was in Bridget to say, 'Why don't you?' but she stayed her tongue. 'And not come back,' she breathed instead, 'like I've done.'

'Yes, go and stay clear of the Curragh for ever.'

'You should. You must have a bit of money put aside.'

Violet hesitated and in this hesitation Bridget saw the change. Whereas before Violet without reservation told her all, she now held back.

'Here she is ...' Violet said.

Bridget tensed and strained her ears to listen, hearing the soft fall of feet on the grass.

When she stepped through from the darkness, her breath a vapour of alcohol, dress crinkled and muddied in patches, Peggy said, 'Well, look who it is – the runaway herself.'

Bridget lowered her eyes to the fire and Peggy mistook this for a sign of remorse, of defeat and dejection, and perhaps if she were sober she might have softened a little and shown some restraint but her face hardened and she was on for pressing home a cruel advantage. Her foul litany exacted neither rebuke nor look from Bridget. When she was breathless and wordless Violet gushed, 'Bridget has money for us.'

'Widow money, I'll wager.'

Bridget snapped, 'Widow money is right. What of it?'

'Do you know the police were out asking me all sorts of questions? They thought I did it. "No," I says, "youse'd want to be looking for the one who's done a bunk and not someone like me who stuck put."'

Silence, apart from the scratchings in the dark, the hiss of a spark, and Violet's loud intake of breath; silence.

Bridget said calmly, 'It was you who told on me – gave them a sure name?'

'I did and what of it? I wasn't taking the blame for it and, sure, up you'd went without saying a kind word to me. Feck you, I said to myself.'

'So it was you who told on me.'

Violet said in a low voice, 'How much have you for us, Bridget?' She tugged feebly on the side of Bridget's skirt. But Bridget didn't notice. Slowly she raised herself.

'Don't get in my face, ya mad oul bitch, or I'll give you a hiding you'll never forget,' Peggy said.

The mongrel got to its paws and this sudden movement in the corner of her eye caught Peggy's full attention.

Violet, her voice fused with rising alarm, said, 'Bridget, don't!'

'Don't what?' Peggy said as she turned to face the pair.

The ladle landed full force across Peggy's crown, the impact bending the handle. Stunned, blood seeping, sieving through the fingers she had involuntarily rushed there, her knees wavered. Bridget gripped a brown ale bottle and brought it down on Peggy's head and then again and once more. Peggy fell onto the fire, knocking over the pot of stew.

'She's burning,' Violet cried, 'get her off it; help me!'

But Bridget was upon Peggy before her, striking her again and again. Sobbing as she punched with the weapon, gnarling and muttering, losing all reason – just hitting out ferociously at Peggy and all else that was within herself to bash, not stopping till the bottle cracked and broke, its loud fracture pulling her eyes to its jagged edge.

Chapter 32

THE RAPPING on his window was long and continuous, almost without punctuation. Vaguely aware of his slow swim to consciousness, his mind was comfortably hazy, lacklustre in identifying the din. Then a flash of memory shook him. Immediately picturing the bag of treasure under his bed, he opened his eyes to the darkness.

A raid! Jaysus, I'm done for, he thought.

'James....'

His name breathed as though by a ghost. The whisper was soft, filled with pain and great disturbance.

He threw his feet to the wooden floor, leaned over and pulled up the sash window that looked out on the main county road which divided the military camp. He smelled rain in the hard wind that blew into his room. Perfume, too. Not at all unpleasant but ineffectual in disguising a bad body odour. This one he hardly knew to talk to although he had lain with her twice in the furze. 'Violet!' he said. 'What are you at, coming here? If the picket sees you on his rounds –'

'James. It's Peggy – something terrible has happened; you have to come.'

'What's happened to her?'

'She's dead. '

Violet was grey-faced, her eyes bulging with terror.

'Okay, move yourself on up on the road – I'll follow.'

He put on his jacket and brim hat and carried a lantern and a short staff. She waited for him at the first patch of furze and they walked to the nest in the pool of weak light cast by his candle. She panted hard, like her lungs had gone too small for such exertion and every so often she bled a sigh and burst into a swell of crying that touched his heart but not enough for him to consider touching her to lend consolation. Touching costs, he remembered a wren telling him.

He saw the fire, almost snuffed, and leaving Violet behind strode purposefully to the prone Peggy.

'Merciful God,' he said, 'who did this?'

Her face had been crushed to a pulp. His stomach heaved.

'What animal did this?'

'Her face ...' Violet said over his shoulder, shakily.

She had no face. 'Who?'

'Bridget.'

'She's away; it can't be –'

'Back, she's back.'

'Since?'

'This evening.'

'Feck.'

He panned left and right, stared into the nest, 'Where is she?'

'She wandered off, James – up she went after doing the harm as if there was something out in the blackness calling her.'

He walked six feet in this direction and six feet in another, as though pulled thither by his thoughts.

'What'll we do, James?'

He was already under suspicion for being involved with the wrens. He had been seen talking with Peggy earlier in the night.

'Get your things,' he said.

'What?'

'Go and gather your things.'

When Violet was gone he reached down Peggy's bosom for her money bag – it held a few coins – business was bad or the gentleman she was with had been good for terms of credit. He looked at the pulped face, felt a rise of bile in his throat and subdued it. She had met with considerable and unbridled force.

Bridget.

He crossed himself and said a Hail Mary.

When he finished and there was no sign of him stirring, Violet said quietly, out of fear that her voice might break the brittle air, 'James.' He nodded and murmured, 'We'll go.'

She had little to bring: a brown canvas bag. 'Where's Peggy's hiding hole?' he asked, getting up from his hunkers, knee joint cracking.

'I –'

'She told me that you knew.'

Head full of beer or not, he was now mighty awake.

'I'll show you,' she said. Violet seemed resigned to him but truly she was in despair at how Peggy's true worth was viewed – in what she'd left behind and not the person she had been. Yes, she thought, Peggy had a temper, but she was caring too if you kept to her right side. James' prayer was a functionary thing he did; he may as well have kept his trap shut for the paltry sincerity that was in it – he couldn't prevent his dislike of her from showing.

A red velvet bag and in it five sovereigns, a gold ring, a pair of brooches, a pendant, a gold necklace and another of pearl. Sepia photographs in rusted iron frames. A nice little booty indeed, apart from the portraits.

He tucked the bag inside his jacket pocket.

'She'd have liked me to have some of it,' Violet said, surprised to find herself saying it.

He stared at her. 'Okay, but I want you off the plains – now. If they come along they'll be badgering you for information and if truth gets out about me I'll have no job, and you could end up in gaol for doing the killing. 'Tis your word against Bridget's, remember.'

He gave her a sovereign and the brooches. Her hand was still held up even as he tied up the bag's laces.

'What?' he said, knowing well what she wanted. He uncinched the knot, dug in for the portraits and gave them over.

A slight rain began to fall. The wind near took his hat and he had to battle to save it from being scurried into the bushes.

'Thanks,' she said.

'Away with you, now.'

'Where will I go?'

'How do I know – just get away from here.'

'Bridget?'

'I'll deal with her.'

When he returned to his room he swept his eyes around for a spot to hide his gains. He was a man who did not like what he owned in life to be far from his grasp. He stood there with the rain drying into him thinking about what he should do – the stuff had to be hid, new and old, for if it was found in his possession it would give people the opportunity to do as they wished with him. He crossed the yard to Kennedy's office, his mind on the wooden ceiling slat near the corner which had been loose for as long as he'd worked as a Ranger. If his treasure wasn't safe hidden in the loft, it'd be safe nowhere; he'd often heard it said that the best place to hide something was under the nose of the very person most likely to go searching for it. He stood on a chair, pushed the two bags through and sat them away at the reach of his arm, across a rafter.

'Who's to know?' he said. 'Who's to bleddy know now?'

He did not sleep when he returned to his room. He wanted a drink and enjoyed the last draws of a bottle of brandy, wishing there was more to see him to the break of day. Bridget had to be found and quickly. You wouldn't know what a one like her would say to the wrong ears, he thought, ones only too eager to believe the worst about people, true or false.

When the first creaks of light penetrated the skies he saddled the piebald and mounted up, pushing the pony forward to the gates. He was startled to see Kennedy strolling through into the yard. He had lost some weight and didn't yet look out of the woods.

'You're in to us early,' James said.

'And you're away as early.'

'Errah, there's no sleep in me and there's reports of dogs moidering sheep.'

'How are things otherwise?'

'Fine – are you up to the ride to come with me?'

'I won't – not today.'

Kennedy passed by into the office, to a dead stove and a hill of paperwork.

The day of it, he thought that evening, entering the tavern, wanting a feed of ale and steak in him. Tired, too – worn to the bones. He espied Violet. He looked twice. It was her. His surprise turned to annoyance.

He went to her table and sat, looked around to see who might be looking at them. A girl who was with Violet left after his gaze had invited her to excuse herself.

'Didn't I tell you to be on your way, Violet?'

'I did nothing wrong, James.'

'Still, you were a witness and a witness can sometimes come to be viewed as an accomplice. After all, you stood by and let the murder happen.'

She thought about this for seconds, then said, 'Bridget is in the workhouse. I'm just after hearing.'

'And who got her there but me? Wandering the plains the morning after her evil deed, jabbering shite nonsense to herself.'

'So that's another thing, isn't it?'

'What is?'

'You want me out of here so I won't be codded into blabbering and yet she'll be staying.'

'She's a lunatic – the eyes in her, piercing. No one heeds the ramblings of a lunatic.' He stabbed the table with his forefinger and said, 'God, you're one thickeen.'

'I am not. I just don't know the right thing to do.'

'The right thing to do was for you to get out of here.'

'You've done well out of warning us and delaying getting us off the plain.'

'We both did well out of the arrangement. Did we not?'

'The going would make me look guilty in the eyes of others.'

He tore at an itch in his scalp. Shook his head. She trusted him not an inch, thinking he might swing her as the murderer.

'Go to England, Violet, or Scotland – if you remain here they'll wear the truth out of you and I'll be brought into the mix, too … I could lose my job, like I've already told you, and be living in the furze myself. You and me and Bridget – we'd be in the shite, the lot of us. Her for killing and us for helping her conceal the fact.'

These points made some sense to her. Especially the latter one – she nodded slowly like his piebald lowering into his nose sack.

'Okay … I'll go. I'll go, James Greaney.'

'You forget all that business now. Take the boat and leave this bed of troubles behind. Change your name. Lose yourself.'

'Okay.'

He said, 'Tonight?'

She sighed and said yes and then he asked if she'd dine with him and perhaps afterwards say a sweet goodbye to him. His itch could wait to be fixed.

'No,' she said.

'No?'

'I'm going now. This moment.'

He watched as she gathered herself, fixed her clothes and crossed the floor to the door. Her female companion hurried after her. Something in him wanted Violet back, to stay a while, to hang close. It was a voice lost out to the drawling tone of the barman saying, 'James, lad, the same as usual?'

The same brimming tankard.

CHAPTER 33

IT WAS late in the evening of the next day that Bridget's thoughts started to filter back to her. She saw the scene unfold before her.

She snuffed a flicker of remorse by welling up within her a deep pool of self-righteousness. Peggy had it coming, she said to herself.

Bridget was in a long and narrow room, women and children around her. The beds were sacks of foul straw, the walls the ash-grey of a spent fire and the ceiling high as though raised there by the hacking coughs of the occupants.

'You're yourself,' said the woman beside her.

'Myself?'

'Oh Jaysus, the glazed look in your eyes when you came in was unnatural and frightening to look at.'

'When was I brought in?'

She remembered Greaney – his words to her hard and thick with poison. But when had he led her here? What had he said to people?

'Yesterday – by your man, Greaney. He and a jarvey did the honours.'

Her throat felt like it had been soaked of all moisture. A scum lined her lips.

'I'll send one of the childer to get you some buttermilk – the water's like piss.'

'Ah, you're a dacent skin.'

'We have to look out for each other in here.'

'So, this is the workhouse.'

'It is – twenty-three bodies of woman and child in here and

twelve beds and most of us sickly. I fought mighty hard to stay out of here. Yet here I am.'

Bridget closed her eyes. A great weariness came over her. A tiredness she'd never before experienced.

'Are you with us?'

Bridget came awake and looked at the small woman with the brown hair and worn out round face. She held up a tin mug of buttermilk.

'Go wet your whistle,' she said.

Bridget thought of the ladle as she took the mug in hand. Her hand got the tremors and she brought the other over to steady it. The murdering hand has the shakes.

The woman's name was as her own and she talked a lot of the terrible deed on the Curragh.

'… that poor unfortunate, beaten to death – they say the face was bet off her. I hope they get the bleddy beggar who did it, a curse on him and all to do with him is what I say.'

She had a squeaky little voice that Bridget found irritating.

'They brought me here,' Bridget said.

'You were found wandering the plains like a blind sheep – up near the military cemetery, so I heard your man Greaney telling the boss here.'

She sipped at the buttermilk.

'Was anyone else brought in here?' Bridget asked, thinking of Violet.

'No. Only you – the last woman brought from the Curragh before you was a young one – she had the coughs fierce bad.'

Full of bother, Bridget thought, where's Violet got to? It's merely a matter of time before the truth spills. I'll be for it then. Unless… Unless I spake up before anyone else does.

The door opened and when her eyes lit on the new arrival the mug fell from her hands.

'Oh Jay! Never mind,' said the other Bridget, 'we'll fix you up.'

Bridget climbed to her feet, her spine inching along the height of the wall.

'Rosanna!'

Chapter 34

ROSANNA HAD heard of Bridget's arrival and went to her though the doctor said she was not to leave the bed. The fleas and ticks can come with me, she said, and he stroked his beard and looked at her like she was a lost case. Giddy-kneed and as light-headed as she was, determination and a hand walking along the wall aided her to the sick room. The matron stood in front of Rosanna to block her progress, her uniform as starched as herself, but stepped aside when the doctor said it was okay. He had to say it twice as though the matron were a stubborn nail that wasn't keen to comply with a hammer.

The women hugged and Bridget said it was awful what happened and though Peggy was a bad bitch she didn't deserve that, did she now?

Rosanna said, 'She did not, for sure. What happened, were you there?'

Bridget brought a deep breath into her and said, 'I saw it all. Greaney, he killed her.'

Rosanna wondered at this for she had spoken to James when he called in to visit her after seeing to Bridget. He did not look unduly disturbed. He had taken her locket and chain for safekeeping and had brought it back thinking that it would be buried with her. 'But here you are, improving by the day, blooming like a beautiful red rose. As pretty as your mother in the locket,' he'd said.

Flatterer he may well be, but James is no killer, she thought.

'Away from here – away from the fecking ears – and tell me,' Rosanna said.

They went to a corner and spoke.

'I thought you were dead,' Bridget said.

'Everyone thought I was – I'm not out of the woods yet, they tell me. I have a fierce weakness and my lungs are fecked but I tell you one thing, as soon I'm some way fixed I'll be out of here, back to the Curragh and unless they burn every furze on the entire plain it's there I'll stay.'

'He did it; he killed Peggy.'

'Not James, surely?'

'With my own eyes I saw it.'

'He did not.'

Bridget sighed and with some vexation pointed to her eyes.

'Over money he said she owed him. I swear on all that's holy.'

'Janey – it's hard to believe.'

'Isn't it just? Beat her in front of my eyes. Like I used to wish to do to her myself but never had the courage.'

'Oh sure, I wanted to murder her too – I understand it all, but James? Ah, no … he's sound, he is.'

'When his temper is even,' Bridget said coldly, panicking inside that she had failed to convince with her story at its first outing.

Rosanna asked herself why James would bring a witness to his crime to this spot and keep her alive? It made little sense. Two dead wrens in the furze would tell no tales. Though she could put her foot through the hole in Bridget's story she decided not to say a word. She needed to speak with James. Her fingers went to her locket. She could not match the fact that James had returned an item of value to her with a man who would draw blood over money.

She took several steps back as though she wanted to get a fresh look at Bridget from a different angle. Something in her retreat appeared to grow a thousand suspicions in Bridget's eyes. Rosanna thought, now's there a slant to Bridget I never saw till now, the look of a fox mapping its way from behind a shelter of furze.

She felt a cough coming on, her energy sapping and said, 'I better be going before I collapse in on myself.'

'I'll give you a hand.'

Rosanna said, 'I'll make my own way. 'Tis the best way in this world – to lean on no one only yourself.'

'As you think yourself, Rosanna – God love you.'

Rosanna had more to say but had not enough strength to speak her mind entirely with Bridget. James had better watch out for himself.

CHAPTER 35

THERE WAS a letter from London. Josie brought it to Richard's room where he had retired for the afternoon to rest himself. Last night had been a most difficult one for him: lying in his bed, candle snuffed, staring into the darkness and the matter with darkness is this: it tells you nothing about who and where you are. Is it so with death? he wondered. The darkness, the creaks of floorboards, soft whisperings of people on the landing, the sound of falling foot-steps on the street, the dying scent of candle smoke. Are the dead haunted by such ghosts? A shallow sleep had brought him no answers.

'Thank you,' he said, looking up from his mahogany desk, cov-ering a scratch he had put there by accident. The small things that we hide.

'Shouldn't you be in your bed?' Josie said.

'I've just this minute got up.'

'You are to persist in going out?'

'I am.'

'I'll have Lynch ready.'

He reached out and took his cousin's hand and squeezed, 'You've been most kind to me, Josie.'

She rested a hand on his shoulder, the light landing of a bird on a thin branch, and said, 'Yes, and why not?'

She turned then and left the room, the door closing out with the faintest of clicks so as not to impinge further on his train of thought. He looked through the window at the narrow street and saw a dog raising its leg to a downpipe and a small, barefooted boy leaving the house of a married man who was known for having boys in his house whenever his wife was away. Again, his thoughts pierced: What is it to you? You won't be around for much longer. Certainly not long enough to finish whatever it is you're of half a mind to commence.

'Tidy your affairs,' spoke the physician, a man in his seventies who was the unhealthiest-looking specimen of man that Richard had ever set eyes on – in contrast to the healthy one that stared back at him during his morning ablutions. Ostensibly healthy, that is.

The rain fell steadily. He reached for a letter-opener and read Mr Dickens's letter: a general enquiry concerning his current work and when he might see it; he'd like it for an edition sooner rather than later. And mention of another assignment, a fee scratched in that lovely, articulate handwriting.

He read the letter again and then put it down. Paris. To work on a story about children who live in the sewers of the city. *Ah well* …

He dipped his quill in ink and wrote to his employer, outlining his progress and recent developments. He would dispatch the story to him presently. Regarding the fee for the new article, that was generous and thus acceptable, but …

Divulging the fact of his terminal illness on a personal level was not to be.

The rain became substantial on their way to the Curragh. The hood was raised but the wind had a slant that carried the rain to their faces. Skies dark and darker again to the west. The mountains to the east blind even to his hard squint.

'I'm going for a sip,' Lynch said, after he reined to a stop outside the yard. 'I shan't be too long.'

'Neither shall I, please God.'

He walked across the yard, avoiding a fresh mush of horse dung, and went straight through the open front door. He knocked on a counter that had a drop leaf raised next to the window. He rapped on the roughly hewn wood and heard steps coming towards him from an adjoining office.

A hostile-looking character indeed, this. Unshaven.

'I'm looking to speak with the Head Ranger, Mr Kennedy, I believe.'

'He's not here. He's been poorly and is in and out of work.'

'Oh.'

'I don't expect to see him till next week. But he could show his nose the second you're gone.'

'And you are?'

'James Greaney – Deputy Ranger.'

'Can you speak with me on the matter of this recent murder of a young woman?'

'I've said who I am – who are you?'

Richard said his name and profession and apologised for not introducing himself in the first instance.

'I suppose I can. But I don't know very much – no one does.'

'Someone must – the murderer, for instance.'

'Well, that does go without saying.'

'Did you know Peggy?'

'I did, of course, a fiery woman – always ready to scrap. Eager for it by-times.'

'She lived alone or so it appears.'

'Sir, that's right.'

He did not like this Greaney. He does not maintain eye contact and his hand goes to his face too often; either the itch is bad or it is a subconscious reaction to a mask that keeps slipping.

'Is that not strange?'

'What?'

'For a nightwalker to live alone in a nest?'

'I've known it to happen. Some of the women would be made outcasts by their own for one reason or another.'

'And hers was the last nest on the 5,000 acres?'

'It was, that we know of, but there'll be more in the summer; they'll spring up all round. We'll get the wrens off it bit by bit with the new laws and heavy fines – I doubt when they go this time if they'll ever be back. But who is to know for sure?'

'Hmm.'

James bridled at the inquisitiveness of this fellow but more so at his stance and how his eyes seemed to lick over every word James spoke, as though tasting it for strength of truth.

'You were at the spot where she was done in?' James said.

'I was. I visited there yesterday.'

James noted the other's hands: soft hands that had never known dirty work.

'I had a drink with her the night it happened. I spoke to the police about it and gave them the name of the fella she left my table to go see.'

'He's innocent. It's been proven.'

'It seems she left the shebeen on her own … I was gone before her.'

'Her head was badly beaten in. Her body partially burned.'

'The boss told me – he found her. He was out himself that day, a rare one for him, and he came across her, lying beside the ghost of a dead fire.'

'And the sight shook him.'

'It still shakes him. He wasn't meant to be out because of his health, but he took it upon himself.'

'Have you any notion as to who would have done such a cowardly thing?'

'There are many soldiers in camp – perhaps one of them.'

'Do you traverse the plains most days?'

'On horseback, most days; it's part of my duties.'

A press man, he says, and he asking questions like he were a judge. Should I be talking to the likes of him at all? Maybe – an un-willingness to talk about the affair might be a clue to all that I'm hiding something.

'James, did you visit Peggy's nest?'

'On a few occasions.'

'To run her?'

'Yes, to try and persuade her to leave before force would be used.'

'And you never saw any other wrens there?'

James shook his head.

Richard had the impression that the man was lying. He was not often wrong when it came to judging a person's character. This fel-low was not coming across as being right in himself.

'Violet?' he said.

'Ah God, Violet left her about a week before the bad act … she could no longer stand to be in Peggy's company.'

'Why do you think she was killed?'

'Over money, perhaps, or saying bad things to someone who had no money or was not able to perform the manly duty. For say-ing the wrong thing to the wrong person at the wrong time – that is what I would wager.'

'A man did for her?'

'I assume. Her head was … the force had to be strong.'

'The constable found a dented soup ladle in the bushes – a sturdy utensil with spatters of blood and strands of hair and other matter on it.'

'God save us all.'

'A man would use his fists, would he not?'

'Not if he didn't want to mark his knuckles.'

'In such a rage I doubt if he would stop to think – no, I believe it's possible that a woman killed her. Possible but perhaps not very likely.'

'I have no firm idea myself.'

Richard rubbed his lips and then the back of his head.

'What's troubling you?' James said.

'Do you know Bridget Lyons?'

'I do.

'I'm going to speak with her within the hour.'

'All this keeps your feather busy, no doubt.'

'It does, indeed.'

'She's a talker – loves to talk.'

'Actually, I think she killed Peggy. Or perhaps she and Violet.'

James' head recoiled a little at this new trail. 'Ah, no. Not Bridget, nor Violet – two unfortunate creatures, yes, but not spillers of blood. No, sir.'

Well, Richard thought, he has not fallen for that little ruse – if he'd readily agreed with my suggestion then I'd be convinced of *his* guilt. As it stands he agrees with my own sentiments, the duo are innocent and unfortunate.

'What makes you think this of the wrens?' James said.

'A little bird sent me word,' Richard said.

A wren, James thought. Sure, that could only be Rosanna? Has Bridget spoken to her? Admitted her guilt? I ought to visit the pair, for my head will go into frenzy from all the guesswork. Or maybe I should just get the hell away from here.

CHAPTER 36

ROSANNA WAS walking by the door to the small room that served as a church in the workhouse. It was the last room at the end of a corridor that led out to a gravel yard and the dead house. An adequate diet, medical treatment and continuous wearing of warm and dry clothes had brought her along but not by much.

There was a wheeze in her lungs and a chill in her back that would never entirely abandon her, and the years she had in store for her had been much lessened by her former lifestyle, short as it had been. The doctor had been blunt and she had been equally so; she would be returning to the Curragh; she had it in mind to build herself a nest near to Samuel's grave – stronger, drier; she had a little money and she would find work and James could keep an eye out for her and the skullers wouldn't want no truck with a woman carrying the disease. Or would they? She thought of the scene she and James had witnessed – no mention of it in the newspaper at all and yet Peggy's death was there in big, bold letters.

Maybe 'twas so because in the soldier's case his body was not found and Peggy's was. Those were her thoughts when she saw Bridget sitting at the end of a pew awaiting her turn to enter the confessional. She was momentarily frozen by the image.

She went to her.

'Bridget, what is your game? Do you know who is in there?' she whispered.

'I do.'

'How could you? You know what he did to me.'

Twice she had met the priest and twice she had stared at him till his eyes dropped. Not even when his fingers clenched and unclenched by his side, as though he were praying for his Jesus to bestow a whip between his fingers, did she blink. There was a kick in her tummy that could only have come from a phantom.

'Rosanna, leave me be. I don't want to live out in the open anymore. I want a roof and a wall between me and the wind and rain.'

Rosanna said, 'He near killed me and he killed Samuel.'

'That's your business.'

'I thought we –'

'We what?'

'We were close.'

'We have nothing; your baby wasn't even born and you should be counting your blessings that he wasn't brought into this feck sake of a world.'

Though Rosanna's slap across the face left a reddening mark, Bridget did not so much as flinch.

Over tea an hour later she saw Mr Richard and Bridget in discussion, then Bridget was brought to an office to speak with a constable and the gentleman, looking about in a semblance of one lost as to what he should do with himself, saw her, smiled and walked to her. A fine-looking man in his green jacket, holding his top hat by the rim, fingers long pale strips of kindling.

'Rosanna, you look radiant,' he said.

She had the big kettle in her hands and poured him a tankard of tea.

'What has you here?' she said, directing him to a table that was empty, away from the others that were nearly so.

'Bridget,' he said. 'There is a development in Peggy's murder.'

'Has she laid claim to it?'

'No,' Richard said.

'Then, who's to blame?'

'Well she has given me a name and I've passed on that information to the constable.'

'James.'

He looked at her, 'How well do you know him?'

'Enough to know that he is not a murderer.'

'Perhaps you are right. I do not know what to believe.'

He spread his hands on the table, 'So, will you stay here?'

'Divil a fear of it.'

'Where will you go?'

'More tea, Mr Tone?'

She saw in him that he had given up on her and was in no mood to proceed further in his desire to improve her welfare. She felt an inexplicable relief at this.

'Are you living with us Irish for ever, Mr Tone?'

'I leave in two days.'

'So do I.'

'Yes,' he said.

She thought that he was a bothered man, weighted down by matters.

'Rosanna?' His voice was stern. 'I called your name twice but you were distant – your thoughts were deep.'

'Deep, indeed, yes,' she said.

'Share them if you would like.'

'That tea of yours is going wild cold.'

CHAPTER 37

BRIDGET'S CHEEK stung and it burned, but no matter. Fire from Rosanna's soul.

The confessional smelled to her of the sour clothes and breath of the woman who had kneeled in here before her. An oniony stink too. She studied the grille and behind it the black board that would slide away to present her with the shadowy profile of Father Taylor. It happened and the eyes, after glimpsing her to grab recognition, were averted. Like stones cast aside. He had her where he wanted her now. A sinner to mould. And unless she submitted herself to the priest and showed him respect and a hunger to repent he would not think twice about hammering it into her. Bridget knew he also wanted something from her, to hear the words of the murder from her mouth. A test to see would she tell him all that he already knew.

'Bless me, Father, for I have sinned grievously,' she said.

'Ah, Bridget, indeed. It's a surprise – a welcome one – to see you in here. How long is it since your last confession?'

'Shame on me, Father, but it's a long time. Too long.'

'You want to confess to your life as a fallen woman, to repent and seek God's love, forgiveness and mercy?'

'Yes, Father. I want only to do good from here on in.'

'How long are you in the workhouse now?'

'Six days, Father.'

'God's grace and forgiveness is not beyond you if you are serious about your intentions.'

'I am, Father. I promise to throw myself on your mercy and God's.'

'I see. Well then, let us begin.'

'I stole, Father.'

'From the widow, is that correct? The poor woman with the one eye?'

'Yes, Father.'

'And you ask for forgiveness of this sin?'

'I do beg, Father.'

There was a lengthy pause that alarmed her; her heart felt as though it were gripped by fingers of ice. Remember this boyo, who he is – flaked skin off Rosanna, he did.

'Is there more that I should know, Bridget? Now is the time – I can't bring anything said here to anyone else's ear. I speak specifically of a murder on the Curragh – if you know anything of it, you must report it to the authorities. If you wish to begin a new life you must shed yourself of your past one. The judge might be lenient on you when it comes to the business of the theft. Constable Walsh has spoken with me ...'

'Father ...'

'Yes?'

'Such is my reputation that no one would believe a word of what I say. They think I'm a liar – and I *have* lied, Father, and I have stolen, and I am a fallen woman – who'd believe me?'

'You wouldn't dare to lie here, to me, in this small chapel, in a place that's going to make you wholesome? This little booth is God's temple.'

'My bad days are behind me, Father.'

'If I listen to you and see fit to instruct you to speak with the law on what you divulge, what will you do?'

Bridget held her breath and then said that she would put aside her fears on the matter and do as bidden out of respect for the gentleman priest.

'Well, speak ...'

Chapter 38

THOUGH IT was two weeks to Christmas, the snow landing heavily and blanketing the ground, Rosanna insisted on staying on in the furze nest within sight of the hawthorn. James had helped her scoop out the earth, trim the briars, build a low wall of turves and gorse. For furniture she had an ammunition box for her few possessions: three saucepans, some crockery, candles, a perforated pot that she set on the fire at night, baby clothes she'd bought for no reason only to hold.

Her bedding of straw she pushed to one side during the day and upturned pots served as stools for visitors, who were rare: James, a girl called Jenny who stayed for two nights and another from Kildare who visited a couple of times bringing some eggs and a loaf of bread. She was that rare sort: one who'd married herself out of trouble and was fond of saying that she knew Rosanna's circumstances too well and could never forget.

The smoke and the cold were not doing her health much good, James thought on his way to see her. But who could blame her for refusing to stay put in the workhouse and having to tolerate breathing the same air as the God man who had flayed her and killed her baby, smothering her world, her dream? This she'd said to him and his heart turned sore because of it. He tied the piebald to a branch of furze and announced his arrival to the nest by calling her name and mentioning his. She looked up at him and passed him a bowl. He lowered himself to an upturned pail and sipped at the potato soup. He drew the back of his gloved hand across his lips, leaving behind a thread of wool that he knew, if he did not remove it, would be swallowed and would give him a cough. He put the bowl on the raw earth and removed his gloves, fingered away the wool and wiped it on the side of his trousers.

'Put them close to the fire, James.'

'For what? They'll soon be wet again.'

'Please yourself.'

'If I get you a little money, would you move into lodgings for a while?' he said. 'Till the snows pass and the March winds give up their whistling.'

Hessian sacking was draped across the doorway and he saw through a flaw in it his piebald, shaking his head when snowflakes tickled his ears. He whinnied and stomped his hoof.

'You're most kind – and where would a man like you get money?'

'I have a small reserve.'

'And not a hoor to keep you going,' she smiled.

He felt himself blush, 'Like I said, I have a little put by.'

'Do you know what they say about the hawthorn, James?'

'That it's a May tree.'

'Aren't you the smart boy?'

'Tell me; you're going to, anyway.'

'It's something Violet told me – that the druids used to worship around it and sacrifice people and have orgies; no farmer will prune them for fear the spirits will torment his luck.'

'Rubbishy oul blather.'

'Who's to say for sure? They say the spirits meet up at the hawthorn tree.'

He clapped his hands together and held them to the fire.

'This nest is a meeting place for the Curragh winds and that's for sure.'

'Will you shush complaining – all I want is to be left alone.'

They were silent for a few minutes.

155

'Will they leave me alone, do you think?' she said.

'They'll tolerate you once you don't make a nuisance of yourself; keep low is my advice to you.'

'I have a low place nearby.'

'Where?'

'The tinker who built it for me said I was never to say, and I can't, James.'

'Suit yourself.'

'Don't take offence.'

'No, I won't.'

'James?'

'Yes.'

'They're going to come for you soon.'

'Who?'

'Don't be stupid, James; you know well.'

'I'm leaving soon.'

'I've told you that Bridget has said your name to them for Peggy's killing. Don't tarry.'

'And they'll sooner listen to a mad thing, do you think, above someone of my station? Hardly.'

'I think they will move against you,' she said.

He stood up, suddenly anxious, realising that Rosanna was right and he had been ignoring his inner voice – as daft as the sheep wandering the land.

'I own great feelings for you, Rosanna.'

'That's kind of you.'

He waited for her to say likewise but the lengthening silence told him that she did not hold him in similar regard. He had hoped that she would not speak of a fondness for him; he knew he'd be wishing to hear more and anything less would be a measure of disappointment not abated by words such as 'friendship' or 'fondness.'

'I better go,' he said.

He made to leave.

'James?'

He looked back.

'Thank you for everything.'

He nodded and walked through, fixed the door of sacking after him. He heard her coughing as he fitted a foot to a stirrup and as he pushed the piebald forward in the snow his mind was in an awful hurry to be away from the plains and the squalid towns and all that was associated with the military – he knew their poisons, their colours false.

The yard and the offices were empty. Kennedy was in work today but away with the Provost Marshal to discuss problems the military were encountering with the sheep farmers. James intended to pack his things and be away with the piebald before Kennedy's return. The boat to England was his best bet and maybe a longer journey from there to the Americas. They say a man can make a fortune in the new world if he is hard-working. He stuffed a canvas bag with some clothes and then went to draw his money and objects from their hiding place. He would sell the piebald easily enough in Dublin.

I'll be set up grand for a while till I find myself passage, he said to himself, removing the bags from the attic, not caring to set the slats right.

It was Kennedy who stopped him in his stride, stepping from a stable with the Provost Sergeant towering at his shoulder.

'James, we've been waiting for you to come for those,' Kennedy said quietly.

James looked from them to the three peelers who had appeared from the roadway, edging toward him. In his head he saw the images of the contents in the bag – and knew – *knew* … He threw the bags at Kennedy and darted back indoors, drawing the bolt across the door, doing likewise in Kennedy's office. He jumped on the desk and punched a hole large enough in the rotting timbers for him to climb through into the attic. His knuckles bled and pained. He leaned his hand to the roof slates and heaved, sending them crashing to the ground. On the roof he eased his way along the slates, the way icy and slippy, the snow making it difficult for him to obtain any sort of purchase – he fell and in the falling he hoped that this was it for him.

Chapter 39

RICHARD HAD sent Lynch to seek out the girl and bring her back to Josie's house, but he returned some hours later and shook his head, adding that he had found the nest but no one in it.

'You looked?' Richard said.

'Didn't I say it?' Lynch said, gripping his cap like he would the neck of a dog that might have bitten him.

'Richard,' Josie said, noticing how upset Lynch was at the insinuation that he had not done his duty.

Richard panned the room,: the shadow of the fire on the busily patterned wallpaper; the hand-embroidered production of a woodland scene on the wall; the over-mantle mirror; his cousin in her bell dress, her hands gripping the rim of the balloon back chair; his luggage of leather trunks waiting to depart.

'I have other news,' Lynch said quietly. 'Someone has asked for you.'

An hour later Richard walked into the cell to speak with James who was manacled hand and foot. His head was bandaged and the blood seeped through in a bright red rosette. There was a purple bruise under his eye.

Richard drew out a chair and sat opposite James at the pine table.

'You have something to tell me?'

'Yes. I sent for you – not just to pay a greeting.'

'I don't have all that much time, Mr Greaney. I'm sailing to London very shortly and the tide waits for no man.'

'I need your help.'

'My help?'

'They're going to hang me.'

'Yes, I'm quite sure that they will.'

'I didn't harm her at all.'

'Bridget Lyons says that you did.'

'She's lying. Why is her word put above mine?'

'You know well why.'

'They gave me that money and the other things in lieu of it …
I used to charge them for rent. It was wrong, I know, but …'

'It's said some of the property was stolen from the nest – that
Peggy found you at her things and, hot-tempered creature that she
was, she went for you.'

'No. Violet was there – she told me that Bridget and Peggy had
words and that Bridget hit her with the ladle. Many times.'

Richard looked at James, the dark smudges under his eyes, the
perspiration shining like crystal through the grime covering his features. He has the same eye as myself – the sort that looks back at
me from the mirror. The look that a death sentence gives to a body.
'Yet you told me that Peggy lived alone – that Violet was absent a
while.'

'I did not kill Peggy. You yourself said Bridget was the killer;
you thought it.'

'I wanted to see what you would say. It was a test, Mr Greaney.'

'Jesus, I am innocent!'

'I would not expect you to say anything else.'

'Bridget did it, I swear to Christ. Listen, listen to me.'

'Did she? A mild-mannered woman like her who'd managed to
live with Peggy for three years without coming to blows … Why
would that happen now?'

'Peggy reported her for the stealing the widow's money. Mr
Tone, they're going to hang an innocent man.'

'I really must be going, James. May God be with you.'

He called for the warder and left without saying another word.

James shouted, 'I didn't do it – I didn't harm a hair on her head! Go find Violet for me. She knows the truth. She can save me.'

Richard stopped. There was silence. He walked on.

'To the port, is it?' Lynch said, as Richard climbed aboard the trap.

'Yes, but stop at the workhouse in Naas for a few minutes.'

The sea was calm, the air bitterly cold. He sat in his cabin and wrote an addendum to his work. The ship's klaxon sounded and there was the phlegm-smothered voice of a sea man berating children for tomfoolery with a sand bucket. He brought his quill from the inkwell and wrote:

Greaney acted as Bridget said he would – he'll protest his innocence to the gallows. There's no sign of Violet, whom Greaney insists will put him in the clear. Bridget stated that both were involved in the killing, that they each took turns in the vicious assault. It was Violet who told Bridget of the murder in strict but drunken confidence. The trial will be swift – perhaps not swift enough. He fed off the wrens' misery and in the end fate spat his badness back at him. He'll swing for it.

I often wonder what became of Rosanna. I like to think that she found sense and has left the plains and is at this moment of writing in front of a warm fire nursing a bowl of broth. But a vein in me is certain that she is dead.

As for Bridget – she is a new person, according to Father Taylor; he is so pleased to see her reform. He has put her to work in the bakery. She loves the heat of the oven. She tells people she is two weeks old in her new life. She gave me an apple pie with cloves to bring on the voyage. I don't believe that the priest has yet retired his riding crop and I wonder if it's that shadow which motivates Bridget into proper behaviour? Perhaps. I said to Bridget that she was the last of the nightwalkers and she said she was and turned her head.

'Yes, me and Rosanna; we're the last of them, I suppose.'

Epilogue

IT HAD stopped snowing. The stars were out and it was freezing. Her brogues scrunched the snow as she moved toward the tree. Near the grave, close to her hidden shelter that she seldom used, she stopped. The branches of the furze drooped under the clothing of snow, touching off her as she advanced along the narrow trail, like she were a dignitary who people would want to touch for the luck it might bring or for having it to say. Her breath hawed the air – there was a comfort in her now, as though all the hurts in her had been blessed away. She kneeled on one knee, removed the locket and chain and kissed it. Next she pushed her hand through the snow, clawed at the stiff earth with her fingertips and placed a dream and a grandmother's love therein.